M000196581

IT'S FUNNY

UNTIL SOMEONE

LOSES AN EYE

(Then It's *Really* Funny)

KURT LUCHS

Sagging
Meniscus

Printed in the United States of America.

Set in Mrs Eaves XL with LaTeX.

ISBN: 978-1-944697-54-9 (hardcover)

ISBN: 978-1-944697-40-2 (paperback)

ISBN: 978-1-944697-41-9 (ebook)

Library of Congress Control Number: 2017949666

Sagging Meniscus Press

web: http://www.saggingmeniscus.com/

email: info@saggingmeniscus.com

Also By Kurt Luchs

It's Funny

Until Someone

Loses an Eye

(Then It's *Really* Funny)

CONTENTS

LETTER OF RECOMMENDATION

To Whom It May Concern:

It is my pleasure to recommend Kurt Luchs for employment at your company. I have known Kurt for nearly six years and I can honestly say that I have not known any other Kurt for nearly as long.

Kurt was with our firm, Pendleton Tool & Die Co., for five and a half of those years. His employment with us ended amicably and by mutual agreement between both parties and the United States Seventh Circuit Court of Appeals. In fact, Kurt was so dedicated that he stopped coming in each morning only when his desk was removed and the locks were changed. Every once in a while, I think I see his face behind a ventilation grille.

During his tenure with us, Kurt held a number of positions reflecting his range of talents and responsibilities: administrative assistant, assistant to the administrator, assistant administrator's aide, administering assistant's associate, and filing clerk. While it would be an exaggeration to say that he performed all his duties, it would be entirely fair to say that he performed them all equally well. In fact there was a consistency and tone to Kurt's job performance that I have never before seen in a living employee—call it an almost supernatural sense of calm. There were times when only a mirror held to Kurt's nostrils would reveal the fiery spirit and pulsing intellect within.

I credit Kurt entirely for inspiring the recent overhaul of our human resources department's background-checking system. His knack for creative self-expression, by which he transformed a three-year stretch in a state reformatory into an M.B.A. from Harvard, was a constant source of amusement.

While some people can be described as "all heart" or "all head," the best way to describe Kurt is "all hands." From a friendly pat on the behind to a friendly pat of butter on the chest, he touched his female colleagues in more ways than most of them had ever heard of.

He was close to his male co-workers, too: in fact, on several occasions it took a stun gun to pry them apart. There were a few who had a hard time seeing Kurt's good-natured roughhousing in the proper light. But in my opinion he never crossed the all-important line between first-degree manslaughter and second-degree murder.

I envy the next company that adds Kurt to its payroll. Why? Because hiring Kurt is like getting a free law school education. You may think you understand the First Amendment, but I'll bet you had no idea that an employee has the constitutional right to emit sudden, piercing shrieks and deafening bursts of profanity near a fellow worker operating an industrial laser.

Kurt also displayed an uncommon willingness and ability to follow instructions—not my instructions but, rather, those he received from the voice in his head.

Kurt's influence on everyone in our company was so extensive that there are still employees who won't start their cars without checking under the hood first. You ask how and why Kurt left our company. Unfortunately, a court order prevents me from sharing all the details. But I can say in perfect candor that I heartily recommend Kurt as a resourceful and indefatigable addition to some other firm. Any other firm.

Sincerely,

Thomas R. Pendleton
President
Pendleton Tool & Die Co.

SPEAK NO EVIL

As almost everyone has heard by now, human beings are not the only creatures to master speech. Certain other primates, principally chimpanzees and gorillas, can also comprehend human language and even learn to talk after a fashion. This is evident both in every session of Congress and in the work of Dr. Jacob Mamoulian, whose experiments prove that apes can form meaningful sentences (which may be one way to tell them from *New York Times* editorial writers). Following are selections from Dr. Mamoulian's scientific journal where he recorded his remarkable discoveries, his hopes and disappointments (and also a fantastic recipe for soy bean nachos).

DECEMBER 31: As the New Year looms ahead I swell with pride and anticipation—or maybe just another case of food poisoning. In any case, I have much to be thankful for. The government has once again demonstrated faith in my research by granting me the funds necessary to continue.

True, they allotted more money to Professor Squelch and his ridiculous attempt to teach a giant squid how to crochet, but I feel my efforts are being recognized.

Today we received a new shipment of test animals as well, and they show much promise. Scrawled on the inner walls of their packing crates were such ambiguous phrases as "White Slavers Must Die" and "Prehensile Power." My less thoughtful colleague Dr. Redvine attributes these signs of pre-verbal instinct to the animals' impatience with the long flight from Africa, while I see in them confirmation of the theories presented in my paper, "Graffiti Among the Higher Primates."

JANUARY 9: Could we be on the verge of a breakthrough already? It happened this morning, after a prolonged hunger strike by the new lab animals. Our college intern Pete Bambino, a strapping youth (his father used to whip him with one), was trying to force-feed a banana to a four-year-old chimp named Gracie when she lost her temper. We would've separated them, but Pete's cap had gotten knocked off and we could hardly tell them apart, until she gave him a slap that sent him spinning like a skater in the Ice Capades and all of the loose change came flying out of his pockets. Then she force-fed *him* the banana. You know Darwin's old saying, "Monkey see, monkey do." Well, none of the 27 apes were happy until they had each slapped Pete and fed him a banana. Some of them did it more than once, illustrating my belief that learned behavior can be just as much fun as instinctive behavior.

Pete, for his part, seemed unhurt but also a little unhinged by the roughing up. He said that he had never eaten so well in his life, and asked his "sorority sisters" if he could live with them now that he had been properly pledged. In short, he refuses to leave the primate compound. On reflection we view this as a stroke of luck, since it means we'll have someone on the inside to gain the animals' trust and demonstrate correct English. Plus Dr. Redvine and I picked up the loose change off the floor and divided $4.68 between us (though I suspect he may have pocketed an extra quarter when I wasn't looking). All in all, a very profitable day for science.

JANUARY 13: To our chagrin the apes have failed to develop any intelligent speech patterns through imitating Pete. On the contrary, they sound exactly like psychology majors. This afternoon, for example, I was administering an oral exam to a young gorilla called Walter to determine whether he could distinguish human speech from a speech given by a labor organizer. He passed with flying colors, but then asked why I was "all up in his face about everything." I stared at him flabbergasted, taut with expectation. Was I about to witness the birth of a new era in human-animal relations? Or was I simply hearing things?

"I am a behavioral researcher," I said as slowly as my pounding heart would allow. "I want to communicate with you."

"Oh, wow," said Walter, forming the words perfectly, glibly, horribly. My heart sank. "I'm really into psychology," he continued. "Pete tells me the finals are a breeze, but I think sociology would totally rock, and besides, it's three credit hours and..." I no longer heard the anthropoid as he rattled off the soul-freezing twaddle of a hardened undergraduate. Why had we not insisted on better controls? I asked myself. Too late, too late. Our only test group was irrevocably contaminated. I felt like crying, but I told Walter the exam was over and waved him away. I forgot my clinical training and sobbed hoarsely, blowing my nose on some litmus paper.

JANUARY 17: We continue to seek ways to inculcate true human speech into our experimental subjects. Letting them watch an address by Vice President Biden was probably a mistake, and the mock classrooms aren't much better. Once again I am troubled by the cultural contaminations, and not just the *Lancelot Link:*

Secret Chimp DVDs they got hold of somehow and showed at an all-night dorm party. And where did the apes pick up texting so quickly? As I was administering a pop quiz, I saw one of them, Charlie, sending this message to a female named Theresa: "u r so 6y! omfg, will u b my bubu?" Naturally I confiscated his cell phone, but how in the name of Jane Goodall can I ever turn back the clock?

JANUARY 25: I have been betrayed by the one closest to me, that foul amoeba Dr. Redvine! Behind my back he has convinced the government that the experiment is a failure, and that the research money would be better spent on his own project of teaching a school of yellow fin tuna to sing the *St. Matthew Passion*. When I discovered his treachery I caught his nose in a pair of calipers and led him to the T-maze where we keep the underfed white rats. It may not have been scientific, but it was very satisfying.

Later I broke the news to the apes that they could no longer count on their student loan deferments. They confided to me that they had planned on "getting into the social media of the streets" anyway, and that they were through with the "old school linear thinking" represented by my laboratory and me. Pete shyly revealed that he had been practicing the accordion and showed me some tin cups and chains he had stolen from a supply cabinet. "These are the true tools of the people," he said. Then, in a moment of unguarded emotion, he slapped me and force-fed me a banana, as did each of the apes in turn. I was speechless.

THOUGHT POLICE BLOTTER

A Bronx branch of the Chase Manhattan Bank was robbed twice yesterday and once this morning in the mind of Andy Scherer, 27. Scherer, a tax consultant, does not own any firearms and has never committed a violent act. Recently, however, he has fallen prey to increasingly savage and vivid daydreams in which he binds and gags the employees and customers of his local bank branch at gunpoint and, after emptying the vault and firing shots that cause mass cowering, makes a spectacular getaway on rocket-powered rollerblades.

At 2:43 a.m. last night, Rosemary Gonzalez, 43, of Deerfield, Illinois, briefly considered setting her cheating, unemployed husband Armando on fire as he slept, but gave up her plan when she realized she was out of lighter fluid and there were no stores open. Her thoughts then shifted to a copper colander she had seen on sale earlier in the day at Crate & Barrel.

Tom Maxwell, 38, of Reno, Nevada, willfully and forcefully generated a mental image of a naked Sharon Stone without the actress's consent, which he then projected onto his wife Patricia as they were having mechanical, partially clothed sex sometime after 10 p.m. last Thursday. The illicit illusion lasted approximately two and a half minutes, after which Maxwell's powers of imagination failed and he fought back an overwhelming desire to weep.

※ ※ ※ ※ ※

Elaine Younger, an administrative assistant at the Oakland Discount Tire Outlet, contemplated stealing a box of blue ballpoint pens, a stack of sticky note pads, and other minor office supplies this past Friday afternoon during her 3 o'clock break. The 51-year-old resident then remembered that she still had not used up the supplies she had filched from her last place of employment. At this point the words, "Oh God, my pap smear results!" flashed through her mind, obliterating all thoughts of petty theft.

※ ※ ※ ※ ※

Robert Michaels once again decided this morning that kidnapping was the only way to resolve in his favor the ongoing custody battle with his ex-wife, Clarice. He mentally rehearsed a detailed plan to abduct his two children, Bob Jr. and Lindsay, from the parochial school they attend in Great Neck, Long Island, going over the fine points out loud with local barman Tony Mendiola. The plan became clearer after the second beer, but somewhat fuzzy after the fourth, and all but disappeared from Michaels' consciousness after the seventh. Michaels, 49, is now resting quietly in the back seat of his car.

A series of highly obscene and abusive calls was nearly made over the past four days by a Gary, Indiana woman who works as a receptionist in the administrative office of Ronald Reagan Elementary. Helen Blossey, 58, came within seconds of making the calls at least several dozen times, being stopped only by incoming calls at the switchboard, which she had to answer. On each occasion, Blossey was prepared to unleash a stream of profanities upon whatever stranger picked up her randomly dialed call. Police have yet to discern a motive.

Randall Gillespie, 31, mentally stalked his coworker, Anne Schwartz, for the eighth time this month in what has become an obsessive evening ritual for the Bridgeport, Connecticut resident. His imagination followed her home after she got off the 5:32 express train two stops before him. He pictured her entering her apartment while he loitered nearby, incorporeal and impotent, unable to mentally enter her home because he had never actually been inside it and thus could not clearly picture the interior.

LEGION OF DOOM

It was madness, I tell you, nothing but madness. Why else would we have followed that slavering martinet Sergeant Delgado over miles of molten dunes into the heart of the Sahara—and us with nothing to drink but our own saliva? And then to come suddenly upon the impenetrable fortress of Nad Elyauq, to fix bayonets and charge its granite walls screaming our lungs out, only to realize it was a mirage, a vapor steaming from our heat-crazed brains—I ask you, were these the actions of healthy men?

But such is life in the Legion. One minute reclining in the Kasbah beneath waving palm fronds as dark-eyed concubines ply you with figs and potent liqueurs; the next minute finding these same sweet maidens have parted your hair with a scimitar.

Like so many others, I first joined the Legion to forget a woman: my wife. In fact, most of the men in my company had enlisted for the same reason: to forget my wife. After a few hellish days of basic training, we had forgotten all about forgetting her and tried instead to forget our tormentor, Sergeant Delgado.

Delgado was a Spaniard, with olive skin and pimento eyes and jaws like castanets. Rumor had it that he was a former bullfighter who had been ejected from the ring for goring a fellow toreador. In the Legion his native cruelty was given free rein, yet he was capable of surprising tenderness and concern for our well-being. Once a private on the verge of starvation stole a crust of bread from the commissary (a serious offense in the Legion,

11

where snacking between meals is forbidden). Delgado assembled us outside the mess and confronted the thief.

"Which is the guilty hand?" the Sergeant asked.

The man held out his left hand, which trembled violently right up to the moment Delgado lopped it off with his saber. As the Sergeant wiped the blade on his pantaloons and turned to leave, the man hissed through teeth clenched in agony:

"Begging your pardon, sir, but the mistake is all mine. I'm afraid my right hand is the real culprit."

The whole company fell silent, waiting for Delgado's customary obscenities and the poor thief's instantaneous decapitation. Instead, the Sergeant wept inconsolably and apologized, accepting all the blame and calling himself "a first-class knucklehead." Then, with infinite regret, he cut off the man's other hand. We were profoundly moved.

We learned the meaning of the Legion motto, "March or Die," by carrying the heaviest military backpacks in the world. Each was a carefully designed desert survival kit containing blankets, sheets, a down comforter, embroidered pillows, an easily assembled four-poster brass bed and canopy, 2000 rounds of ammunition, an extra rifle and bayonet, enough bricks to build a walled fort, two liters of water, eight liters of whiskey, a copper cooking pot, a side of beef, a side of pork, a side of hydrolyzed vegetable protein, two complete extra uniforms and an extra Legionnaire.

A man could march about five feet with this monstrosity on his back—a distance that increased to 50 miles at the point of Delgado's bayonet. To his credit, the Sergeant led us every step of the way, though due to a severe case of corns he had to be carried on a velvet litter while we marched and sang.

Legionnaires love to sing, particularly their theme song, "Le Boudin" (literally, "the blood sausage"). During Maurice Chevalier's little-known enlistment in the 1920s, higher-ups considered changing the theme to "You Brought a New Kind of Love to Me." But then Chevalier was dishonorably discharged for creating an "obscene public display" (he removed the veil from the wife of a local sheikh), and the idea was dropped.

For many, the Legion is the only alternative to a jail sentence. It will overlook petty crimes such as homicide and kidnapping if a man has something substantial to offer—say, a cold case of Coors. It is an open secret that, while the Legion enforces strict prohibitions against practically all other vices, it has no rules against drinking. Alcoholism is indeed the real "Legionnaire's Disease." Moonshine was common. I remember a home-brew made of fermented cactus rinds and camel droppings, with just a pinch of cinnamon for flavor. We would sip this concoction until we saw two of everything, including our paychecks. Then we would cash the extra checks and send the money home to mother.

I hope my remarks have not given the impression that life in the Legion was an unending round of degradation and torture. Far from it! A Legionnaire is as fond of fun as the next man—even more so, for in the Legion the next man is usually maimed or deceased.

Our favorite holiday was the Feast of Camerone, held every April 30. This commemorated the massacre at Camerone, Mexico, in 1863, when Captain Jean Danjou and his force of 46 held off 2,000 attackers, finally perishing as Danjou led the last desperate bayonet charge. To celebrate this brave occasion, Sergeant Delgado organized us into teams of "attackers" (the enlisted men) and "defenders" (Delgado and his staff) and had us re-enact the battle. Strictly speaking, these games were played more according to the spirit than the letter of historical reality. That the "defenders" were armed with real bayonets and the "attackers" only with camel-hair brooms we put down to the Sergeant's innate sense of fair play.

EXCERPTS FROM THE SAFETY BROCHURE

Good morning, and welcome to United Airlines Space Shuttle flight number 909 to Kuala Lumpur and continuing on to the moon base at Copernicus Crater City. Please remain in your seat throughout takeoff and after entering orbit. If you must leave your seat, keep your magnetic boots on and walk slowly and carefully. Do not remove your boots and try to float down the aisle carrying your boots. Do not wait until the head of one of your fellow passengers or a crew member is between your boots and a metal wall and then let the boots go, pretending not to know what will happen.

Under no circumstances should you cover your mouth with one hand, make false radio static noises and say, "Houston, we have a problem." Nor should you fashion a realistic alien pseudo-pod out of phosphorescent Silly Putty and surreptitiously place it on the shoulder of the passenger in front of you. Nor should you make strange gurgling sounds, clutch your heart and yell hysterically, "The little bugger's biting through my chest cavity!"

When being served your in-flight meal, please refrain from asking the flight attendant what went wrong with the food replicators. Do not refer to any crew member as "Seven of Nine" or "Two of 36D," and do not mention, even obliquely, your own "very personal Borg implant." Keep the lid on your drink at all times. Do not attempt to "liberate" your drink from the "unnatural restraints of a weak, contemptible gravitational field." If your drink should accidentally escape from its sealed reverse-pressure container, do not slap the ball of liquid and disperse it into a thousand tiny globules.

If you are seated near an emergency exit, do not ask the flight attendant for an electric screwdriver under the pretext that you are "just one lug nut away from Nirvana." Do not place a holographic decal of a Hubble telescope photo of a supernova on the window and ask your fellow passengers what that strange light is out there. It would also be a mistake at this point to cut a Ping-Pong ball in half, draw scraggly lines on the pieces with a red felt-tip pen, insert a piece into each eye socket and moan, "Oh my God, not that solar flare thing again!"

When the order is given to turn off all cellular phones, laptop computers and portable video players prior to takeoff, it would be considered a serious breach of security to keep pounding the mouseball and screaming, "More thrust, damn it, we need more thrust or we'll never achieve escape velocity!"

Passengers are strictly forbidden to pull down the oxygen masks directly above their seats unless first instructed by a non-imaginary crew member. Further, they are not to breathe into the mask, cough as if suffocating, and declare, "My people need at least a 40 percent chlorine mixture to maintain normal body metabolism." Simulated body spasms and cries for anyone present to erect a level 10 force field and fill it with your world's atmosphere could be disruptive to other travelers.

If you need to use the restroom, it would be best to withhold any loudly uttered comments from within the cubicle along the lines of, "My arm! It's got my arm!" or "Cut it out—that tickles!" Do not bang your fist on the inside wall and issue a warning about the wormhole reopening and the need to reverse impulse engines.

During our final approach and landing, please avoid assuming a head-down crash position atop the nearest flight attendant and imitating an air-raid siren or any type of emergency vehicle or injured seagoing mammal.

If you are unable to read or understand these instructions, do not ask the passengers next to you to read the instructions silently to themselves while you attempt to perform a Vulcan mind-meld.

Finally, we ask that while waiting to exit from the spacecraft, you refrain from any high-decibel outbursts in which you plead frantically for someone named "Hal" to "open the pod bay doors."

We hope you enjoy the flight, and thank you for choosing United on your first day of lunar work-release.

Editorial

We join with all other Americans in applauding the President's recent decision. In light of the volatile situation around the globe we feel it was the only decision he could make and, all things considered, we're glad he made it.

We may not agree with everything he says he'll do, but we'll defend to the death his right to say he'll do it—so long as he doesn't actually do it. In today's world, saying it should be enough.

George Washington said it. We can't recall at the moment exactly what Washington said, but it must have been good because he was that kind of man and once he said something it was said forever.

Nor did he stop there. What he said he'd do he did, and when he did something it stayed done.

Did Abraham Lincoln ever say, "It can't be done"?

Perhaps. Perhaps not.

But if he did he was talking through his beard and no one heard him. And more power to him, we say!

Indeed, a bullet ended his life, as bullets have ended the lives of so many other brave Americans in war and in peace. Some of them also had beards like Lincoln. Some did not. In a few cases, we suppose, the beard may even have been pasted on. A hard, bitter truth, if in fact it is the truth, or at least truth-like, but one this nation would be better off facing squarely here and now.

Or maybe there and later.

Because in the final analysis, isn't that the very picture of a true American: a man who may or may not be wearing a false beard, who may even have forgotten to shave, but who, underneath it all, and taken all in all, is the salt of the earth?

We applaud them all.

Let it be understood that we are not by any means advocating new legislation along these lines, although there are many plausible arguments for it—too many to enumerate here. Nor are we necessarily opposed to such a law, despite the many convincing reasons for taking such a stance—more reasons than you could shake a stick at.

Of course if you did shake a stick at them, at least it wouldn't go "Bang!" and kill three innocent bystanders.

Yet we must ask ourselves, since no one else is listening: Can anyone be said, in this day and age and in today's society, to be truly innocent? Or were they possibly enemies of the state? And if so, which state? If it were Alabama, could we blame them? Or should we applaud them, too?

The issue of state's rights requires careful and serious consideration. Let us merely state that all states have or should have state's rights, that they have the right to state those rights, and that one of those rights is the right to state that state's rights are, by right, those rights belonging only to states.

We don't know how to put our position any more simply than that.

It's only our opinion, but we're prepared to stand firmly behind it, where nobody can find us.

The Kurt Luchs Money-Making System

Dear Ms. Kendrick,

Thank you for your query about your recent order for the Kurt Luchs Money-Making System. Sales have exceeded all expectations and I'm not ashamed to admit that we're struggling to keep up. Rest assured, however, that your video, six audiocassettes and instruction book will be winging their way to you shortly. In the meantime, please accept with our compliments (but not necessarily at our expense) the enclosed bonus booklet, "Kurt's 101 Ways to Use a Metal Detector to Provide for Your Golden Years."

Sincerely,

Kurt Luchs
Sales Manager

P.S. Do you remember in the fine print of your sales contract where it says, "Available now for three (or four) easy payments of $44.98 each"? Well, we've just decided and it's four. To expedite your order please send $44.98 in check or money order today.

※ ※ ※ ※ ※

Dear Ms. Kendrick,

Many thanks for your fourth and final payment for the Kurt Luchs Money-Making System. How does it feel to know that you may soon be richer (or poorer) than you've ever dreamed possible? Do you think you can handle it?

Sincerely,

Kurt Luchs

Marketing Director

P.S. Speaking of handling, I must bring a minor detail to your attention. The Kurt Luchs Money-Making System is indeed sent to all purchasers postpaid, but as it says in the contract, "postpaid (by you)." This is no time to be penny wise and pound foolish, Ms. Kendrick. Send the necessary $14.98 for postage and handling today and we'll throw in a (nearly) free reprint of my award-winning brochure, "Kurt's Secrets for Finding Loose Change Under Swingsets and Couch Cushions."

※ ※ ※ ※ ※

Dear Ms. Kendrick,

I don't know what's holding up your order, but I will do everything in my power to get to the bottom of it. It's your right, seeing as all of our customers are automatically enrolled in the Kurt Luchs Protection Plan, a plan for the protection of Kurt Luchs and, to a lesser extent, any purchasers of the Kurt Luchs Money-Making System. I'm sure I needn't remind you that under this plan you are entitled to a full accounting of why this plan cannot provide you with a full accounting of what you are entitled to under this plan. My wish for you is that you use this brief lull in your account activity to peruse the enclosed photocopy of my latest hard-hitting advertorial, "Returnable Soft Drink Cans: The Key to Your Financial Future?"

Sincerely,

Kurt Luchs

President

P.S. It's a small point but worth reiterating that the Kurt Luchs Protection Plan is guaranteed to be free (or not). It's not. Make sure you are covered by sending $39.98 today by check or money order. Or pay by credit card and save 100 percent on your next three long-distance calls (by not making them).

❋ ❋ ❋ ❋ ❋

Dear Ms. Kendrick,

I'm responding to your last letter in hopes that I can personally straighten this whole thing out and avoid bringing lawyers into it. Let me see if I understand your three concerns:

1. You still have not received the Kurt Luchs Money-Making System despite having paid in full.

2. What you have received is a duplicate invoice demanding payment—again—for your order.

3. A $5000 cash advance has been drawn against your American Express Gold Card at a Mexican bank without your knowledge or consent.

Let me deal with the second concern first. You could simply destroy the duplicate invoice, but to tell you the truth that would really mess up our accounting. Our Accounts Receivable Director (me) is very superstitious about closing out the books each month. I suggest you go ahead and pay the invoice and then let us issue a refund per our standard procedure. The best part about that course of action is that it also addresses your first concern. Yes, technically you have paid in full. But technically our computer doesn't know that. As our IS Director, I can't fix the problem without your prompt cooperation.

I apologize (up to a point) for any inconvenience these misunderstandings may have caused. I admit to being somewhat distracted lately, what with the tripling of our sales and the opening of a new manufacturing and fulfillment center in Tijuana this past month.

Sincerely,

Kurt Luchs
Acting President

P.S. Oops! I almost forgot your third concern. I wish I could help you with that mysterious American Express bill, but I am as much in the dark about this as you are. Are you sure you didn't take a Mexican vacation recently? Next time perhaps you should read the enclosed refrigerator magnet, "Five Dream Vacations You Can Take Right in Your Own Home for Practically Nothing."

❋ ❋ ❋ ❋ ❋

Dear Ms. Kendrick,

I do wish you hadn't gone and done that. What problems between two people were ever solved by a lawsuit? Nonetheless, as your attorneys have requested, I am enclosing a check for the full amount of what you have (possibly) spent on the Kurt Luchs Money-Making System. Considering how tight things are around here lately, and with the sudden closing of our south-of-the-border operation, you'll forgive me for sending this letter postage due.

Sincerely,

Kurt Luchs
Former Part-Owner

P.S. I should mention that by opening and reading this letter you have now received the final lesson in the Kurt Luchs Money-Making System. That will explain the stop payment we have put on the enclosed check, as well as the invoice for additional consulting services that is being faxed to you at this moment.

SMALL TALK

The world is getting smaller—have you noticed? *We* have, and we say, "Keep shrinking, world!" Small is beautiful. Small is affordable. Small takes us inside and *throws away the key.* Smart money says small is here to stay. Dumb money doesn't say anything.

Small means boarding up those big garish picture windows, those achingly obvious views of decay. Small means gazing only through the security peephole—and then only when you're sure there's no one waiting outside the door. Small means being mean, for the fun of it. Keep them waiting. Don't look through the security peephole, not even to smile at how poorly they're dressed. Instead, play that downloaded ambient recording of party noises—drunken laughter, glasses tinkling, cocktail chatter—and don't answer the buzzer. Make them think you're having *one kind of fun* when you're really having *another kind.*

Insiders are saying almost nothing about small. Why should they? They don't want you to know. They want you to keep feeding your fish the *recommended* amount of food, as opposed to a *smaller* amount, an amount that fits *your* needs. You have no idea how silly this makes you look. Try thinking small for a change. Give your fish only a taste of food—a pinch—and you'll notice the difference in them. And in *you.*

Small rugs are *in*—flimsy synthetic rugs that cover nothing, do nothing. Honest rugs that refuse to pretend they can do the job, that slide out from underneath your loved ones, causing them to crack their heads on your exquisitely small nonfunctional plumbing fixtures.

Small drinking glasses are in—have you heard? We thought not. Who would have told you? Smaller shot glasses are *very* in—monogrammed little cylinders of solid glass with a tiny depression at the top to hold the liquor, to be *moistened* with the liquor. Also, slightly concave wineglasses that *spill more than they can hold.* Very in.

Entrees have given way to hors d'oeuvres. Not the fulsome, almost nutritious hors d'oeuvres of the past, but *small* hors d'oeuvres —indiscernible specks at the ends of toothpicks. Specks that cannot be eaten without puncturing the tongue, in a small way.

Wall decorations, too, are smaller, more *focused.* Stuffed mammals and reptiles are out—too big. Also, endangered birds of prey—way too big. But insects are *just right.* Not real insects, of course, but life-sized rubber replicas with hidden suction cups for adhering to the smooth surfaces in your life.

We could tell you where to find them, the places where all the best people are shopping—those in the know. We could tell you.

But we won't.

MANGLERS MALL

Hello, shoppers everywhere, from Manglers Mall! Yes, we're back again, and we've *learned our lesson*. No, please, don't go. Not now. Please. We were wrong. We admit it. The customer is *always* right. We know that now. We didn't know it before.

Before we thought the customer was an unnecessary evil. We thought we could fling boiling water on him and push him into potholes full of hot tar while we looked on, laughing. We believed we could hire thugs to break his fingers, make embarrassing remarks about him in front of his loved ones, stain his virgin wool sweater with beakers of dangerous industrial solvents, and he would still shop at Manglers. We never considered his feelings. *Your* feelings. So you went away. We don't blame you, no, but you screamed—a little too loudly, perhaps—and you went away. In droves. You hid in the forest under mounds of pine needles, afraid to breathe, afraid your own fear would betray you. Some of you changed your names and crossed the border, never to be heard of again.

Things weren't the same here at the Mall. The cash registers grew silent. The colored streamers and tiny plastic flags drooped in the sudden chill. Yes, we had to abandon the furnace, our one source of warmth and delight. No more for us the sound of customers moving their lips as they read the blue neon sign above the incinerator door: THIS WAY ONLY. No more their petulant but docile voices as they climbed inside, still clutching their shopping bags, and the heavy steel automatically clicked shut behind them, their cries fading as they disappeared and the door opened once again and the sign was relit.

Even our cherished mall walkers were gone, the elder ones who walked and walked and looked and looked but seldom bought. Yet such dignity and diversity they brought to Manglers, these superfluous breathers too light to trigger the pneumatic bear traps scattered throughout the food court, too slow to register on the motion sensors attached to the grappling guns lining the mezzanine. In the end the mall walkers finally succumbed to the simple beauty of random laser bursts from the specially enhanced security cameras, and the slow shuffle of Hush Puppies was heard no more.

Then we had to dismiss the guards without notice. We let them go. But they *wouldn't* go. They lived in the ventilator shafts. They became despondent. They let their bright yellow uniforms become soiled, and few of them bothered to shave, although they did clean their weapons. They did that for days. Then, without looking up, they would open fire. At the ground. Into the air. Sometimes they would hit a window, sometimes a manager; it didn't seem to matter. Morale was at an all-time low. We thought you might never come back.

But you did! You were hiding, true, sleeping in shopping carts. We didn't always recognize you when the searchlights caught you unawares at night, blinding you, making you crawl back into the underbrush like frightened sow bugs. But we knew you were out there. We could feel your eyes poring over every Going Out Of Business sign, every Liquidation Sale notice. When men's polyester double-knit slacks were marked down 98 percent, some of you *almost* ventured back into the Mall. You were so close, just inches away, and then the mines began to go off, and you had second thoughts. You decided you could do without our slacks for a while. You settled on one of the cheaper brands, knowing in your hearts all along that Manglers Means Quality, At Prices You Can't Afford Not To Afford.

When we had Damage Discount Days for Ladies' Chainsaws, one woman *did* enter the Mall—by mistake, as it happened. She wasn't a shopper at all! She was merely asking directions. We told her where to go, and as she was turning to leave we set the dogs loose. (The dogs, by the way, are so different you wouldn't know them. They respond only to *commands.* No longer do they take the initiative. Something to consider when you're wondering where to buy.)

We at Manglers take your patronage seriously. We're willing to meet you halfway. We'd be more than happy to disconnect the electro-stun handrails on the escalators if you'd come in—a few of you at a time, of course—to browse. The free balloons are filled exclusively with helium now. You needn't be afraid to smoke. You needn't be afraid at all! We *like* you. We want you to *like* us. So? So come here. *Now*. That's it. Keep moving. Keep your hands in the air. The man in the watchtower will tell you what happens next. The one with the megaphone. Pay no attention to that man behind the curtain.

THE KAFKA CONVENTION

"What do you mean you can't find my briefcase?" K.'s voice rose harshly above the general clatter and muttering at the airport's baggage claim area. It was not the first time he had asked that question that morning. Once more, with diminishing patience, the official-looking young clerk gave his explanation.

"Sir, I've told you all I know. We have no record of your briefcase ever being on board this or any other flight. We show no luggage for you at all. In fact, to be perfectly honest, I don't even find you on the seating chart. Unless you can produce a ticket stub of some kind..." He let the sentence dangle in the air, as if to underscore the nebulous nature of K.'s claim. His bright blue uniform gave him the appearance of a policeman, and for some reason the sight of his shiny but useless epaulets filled K. with a vague apprehension. Nonetheless, K. was shouting and gesticulating wildly. People nearby looked up in curiosity.

"I'm telling you for the last time. My ticket stub is gone, vanished—poof! You understand? Somehow my overcoat became confused with that of another passenger, and I now wear the garment of a Doctor Thomas Mann. See? Here's *his* ticket stub!" K. waved a ragged scrap of pasteboard in the clerk's immobile face.

"If you're suggesting I give you Doctor Mann's baggage, I'm afraid I can't do that either," said the young man, who had already begun to process the papers of the customer just behind K.

"I don't *want* Doctor Mann's baggage, you imbecile!" Without thinking, he had grabbed the clerk by the lapels and lifted him clear off his toes. When he heard another clerk mention calling security, K. suddenly became quiet, almost apologetic. He let go of the clerk's collar and even brushed a June bug off one of his epaulets. "I only want what's coming to me. My briefcase, you understand, no one else's. I'm not looking for any favors, but my briefcase happens to contain the only existing copy of my thesis, which I am to deliver later today at the convention."

"Oh? And what convention might that be?" the clerk said with a sneer that made the other customers titter.

"The K-kafka C-convention," K. stuttered. But for a nearly imperceptible look of horror, the clerk's face remained blank. K. continued with feverish enthusiasm. "Franz K-kafka, the writer. In my thesis I compare him to a variety of intestinal worm, you see, a species whose appetite and capacity for guilt are equally immense. Such parasites usually starve themselves to d-d-death, in a sense."

"To b-b-be sure," mocked the clerk, "but if you'll excuse me..." Everyone laughed but K., who turned red and started to back away.

"Of course, of course," he said. "Never mind me." He stumbled into an obese, unkempt woman who was openly nursing the largest infant K. had ever seen. Despite the sickening bluish tint of the child's skull, K. felt obliged to pat it and say something, however banal: "Nice baby." At that moment the head came up to bite his hand, and K. found to his amazement and repulsion that it belonged not to a child but to a wizened old man with smacking gums. The octogenarian giggled inanely and snatched K.'s alpine hat from his head.

"My hat! Mine!" screeched the old man with delight. The woman removed a large sausage from her handbag and began to methodically beat K. with it.

"Filth!" she yelled.

"Of course," said K. He had backed all the way to the edge of the up escalator, and now tumbled backwards down the sharp metal stairs. He could hear more laughter and what sounded like applause coming from above as he lay crumpled at the foot of the escalator. His face protruded over the moving stairs, and as each new step emerged his chin bounced on it painfully.

"Perhaps if I remain here suffering quietly," K. thought, "the Superintendent of this facility will notice that I—an honored foreigner having received official invitation, no less—am being treated in this scandalous fashion, and will take pity on me. If he is worthy of his office he will be outraged, and with a snap of his fingers he will order that my briefcase be restored to me. Who knows? He may even award me certain damages."

K.'s meditations were interrupted by a piercing pain in his backside. He turned to discover a lean Hispanic janitor trying to impale him on a pointed spike and lift him into a refuse bag. "Stop that nonsense at once, or I'll report you to the authorities! Do you hear?" K. did his best to sound threatening, but his voice had suddenly acquired an odd, squeaking quality. He quickly learned that he had also lost control of his body.

The janitor paused and looked at him oddly. "Hey, Tony, come over here!" he called to another man further down the hall. "You gotta see this! This June bug is at least four inches long, and its mouth is moving almost like it's trying to say something!" K. sputtered and tried to deny the ridiculous charge that he had become an insect, but upon examination he saw that such was indeed the case. He had been flipped upon his back and could only wave his six pitifully thin legs in the air and make a nervous sort of buzz. His speech was no longer comprehensible.

"Pleazzze, help meezzzz! I muzzzt get to zzzee convenzzzion!" The janitors both laughed heartily at these pathetic sounds.

"Man, that's spooky! I don't know what it is, but I think we better kill it quick," said the one who had first noticed K. "Livin' la vida loca, and now your back is broke-a," the one called Tony said as his partner flipped K. over and tried once more to run him through. K. found the peculiar singsong strangely comforting, and did not resist as the man put the sharp spike through the space between his folded wings, lifted him roughly, and stuffed him into the dark plastic bag.

LEGENDS OF THE OOH LA LAS

Of all the folk legends handed down by Native Americans, surely there are none so rich or so varied—or so utterly pointless—as those of the Ooh La Las.

The Ooh La La Indians were quite similar to their distant cousins the Oglala Sioux, in that both were nomadic societies of hunter-warriors with strong shamanistic beliefs. The Ooh La Las, however, were known to cheat at cards, to file fraudulent tax returns, and to wear socks that clashed terribly with their slacks. Often they fished in sacred lakes without buying permits, and in one surprise war raid several hundred were caught driving with expired licenses.

All this led to the Oglala-Ooh La La War of 1481, in which the Ooh La Las territory was reduced from an area the size of Wyoming to several square inches on the side of a crumbling mesa in Death Valley. For years afterward the surviving Ooh La Las—all 28 of them—lived there in a state of peace and plenty broken only by starvation and murderous assaults upon their neighbors and one another. Then the white man discovered valuable deposits of sandstone on their land, and their complex culture came to an all-too-timely end.

Fortunately for anthropology teachers, many of their countless "gokiblu" (dirty stories) have survived, transmitted orally or sometimes by a virus. These rambunctious tales were not meant to instruct or even to entertain, but rather to "jibbegawah" (torment) the listener, much like the television programming of today. Judging from the examples below, they must have been eminently successful.

The Great Spirit

Most Ooh La Las professed to believe in a Great Spirit, the First Cause and Prime Mover of all things, an entity they referred to out of respect as "Mel." Mel was omnipotent, omnipresent and omniscient—which made it awfully difficult to plan a surprise party for him. It was common practice to leave food offerings for Mel; say, a dish of salted nuts, or some crackers and onion dip. In times of trouble a 15 percent gratuity would be added. Mel was said to be the son of Ruth and Irving, but Ruth could never prove it in court.

How the Snake Lost His Legs

This was a favorite tale among the Ooh La Las, along with the one about the three Irishmen. Often when sitting around a crackling fire one of them would begin this story, and then the others would wordlessly toss him into the flames.

It seems there was a hapless hunter called Limping Worm who would neither hunt nor fish and spent most of his time trying to catch horseflies in his hands. One day he was visited by Weasel With the Face of a Former President, who was a very wicked but cunning forest creature.

"Listen, oh foolish one," said Weasel. "If you stand near the edge of the woods at midnight, you will receive an omen that will assure you of good hunting forever."

"How do I know you're not lying?" asked Limping Worm as he absentmindedly popped a horsefly into his mouth.

"I *am* lying, you twit."

"Oh. Well, as long as you're honest about it..."

That night Limping Worm crept to the outskirts of the forest and waited. Slowly the moon set and night deepened around him. He was about to leave when three men in dark medicine masks blocked his way.

"Are you the witless one called Limping Worm?" the biggest of them inquired.

"Why, yes, I am," he began. "But what—"

Before he could finish they beat and kicked him, stole his popcorn necklace and left him to die. A few minutes later he was eaten by a nearsighted bear with a very poor sense of smell.

And ever since that day, the snake has had no legs.

A Vision

One of the oldest Ooh La La legends (stop me if you've heard it) concerns a warrior's quest for his Power Vision, a way of peering into the spirit world without drugs or corrective lenses. The young tribesman sat alone on a hilltop in the wilderness, naked, with no food but a bag of hard candy. He fasted and prayed and chanted Mel's name to no avail. At last he reached into a buffalo-skin pouch and produced a spider as large as his own hand. Placing the dark wriggling form on his face, he let out a scream that shook the saguaro cactuses and echoed in the hidden ravines of the desert. Suddenly he heard a high-pitched whine just overhead, and then a deep, booming voice:

"Look, it's after hours; I'm on straight salary, no overtime. Can it wait until Monday?"

"Oh mighty Mel, give me a vision, that I may know on what path to place my moccasins."

There was a whirring sound in the young man's ears, and then a resounding crack as of an oak tree split in two by lightning. Something struck him on the back of the head, and he fell unconscious to the ground. In his fitful sleep he found himself lost in a nightmare world.

He saw great leafless tree trunks coughing a black mist into the air; he saw pale-fleshed strangers in clinging garments with sports franchise logos embroidered on their chests; he saw some of them hitting their women and torturing their animals; he saw them emerge as one from the hideous square burial mounds where their children sat bewitched by the shifting gray lights from the Box of the Dead Spirits; he saw them willingly swallowed by the Shiny Buffalo That Run Without Hooves, and watched in horror as the growling beasts collided aimlessly and stampeded toward the Village That Eats Its Young, a place of filth and smoke filled with the howls of the dead and the dying.

There the Shiny Buffalo spit up their sickly cargo, and the pale strangers entered the burial towers of their ancestors, which reached into the heavens and must have been crowded with corpses, or so the young warrior thought.

He awoke in a cold sweat and gingerly felt the lump at the base of his skull.

"Oh Mel," he cried. "What means this evil dream?"

But for once the Great Spirit was silent, and the only sound was of a mournful wind sweeping across the prairie.

NATURE'S LITTLE SEISMOGRAPHS

I have here in my hand an article that would cause everyone a great deal of worry if there weren't already so many things to worry about. It seems a group of scientists at UCLA have discovered a new method of predicting earthquakes based on the reactions of the common cockroach *(Blatta orientalis)*. Regardless of what we may think of them (cockroaches, I mean), they are highly sensitive creatures. They've been around a lot longer than us and it doesn't surprise me one bit to learn that they can spot an earthquake coming up to twelve hours away. After that, though, they simply make fools of themselves. They go all to pieces.

According to this article the average cockroach, when he feels an earthquake coming on, "may run in circles for hours and hours until he's completely exhausted, then collapse on his back in a death-like coma." What it doesn't say is that the little fellow is probably screaming "Earthquake! Earthquake!" at the top of his tiny lungs, hoping that some responsible citizen will alert the authorities.

But no one hears him because, after all, no one listens to a cockroach except another cockroach, and even they don't really listen—they just nod their heads and murmur "I know, I know." So he passes out on the floor and usually has to be brought around with smelling salts. That's when the full realization hits him. Many roaches will sit down right then and have themselves a good cry. Others turn to drink, and it's no use trying to talk them out of it. They *know.*

Another sign of impending doom is that the roach "loses all interest in the opposite sex." As soon as he feels the slightest tremor, apparently, the male drops everything and says, "Not tonight, I have an earthquake." There's nothing for the female to do but smoke a cigarette until he gets over it. The female isn't annoyed by earthquakes. She is only annoyed by the male.

What's frightening about all this is that the scientists are willing to pin their future—and ours—on so chronically high-strung an insect as the cockroach. Sure, he gets the jitters whenever he hears an earthquake, but maybe he falls out of bed when a train whistle blows in the middle of the night, too. Maybe any little noise sets him off. He's continually on the verge of a nervous breakdown.

How do we know other, more trustworthy household pests can't be trained to do the same job? I'll bet sowbugs can predict earthquakes just as accurately as cockroaches, yet because they don't go pulling their own legs off and sobbing into their handkerchiefs they never make the news. Instead, they hide under the nearest rock until it's safe outside. Then when they crawl back into the sunlight, dusting off their antennae, they can always say "I told you so."

I say let's give the sowbugs a chance. It's either that or climb under the rock with them.

1040M

1040M U.S. Individual Mafioso Tax Return

Label

Use the IRS label. Otherwise, please print or type, or at least let Luigi in accounting forge it for you.

Your first name and initial _____

Last name _____

Official nickname _____

Home address _____

No, your *real* home address _____

City, state, and ZIP code _____

Pool room where you can normally be reached _____

If a joint return, mistress's first name and initial _____

Last name _____

Illegal campaign contribution

Do you want $10,000 to go to this fund? Yes ☐ No ☐

Note: *Checking "Yes" will not shorten any currently pending prison sentences.*

Filing Status

Check only one box.

1 ☐ Single

2 ☐ Married filing joint return (even if spouse is now part of patio or swimming pool)

3 ☐ Married filing separate return (spouse is nominal head of separate dummy corporation)

4 ☐ Head or member of extended criminal family. (See page 10.)

5 ☐ Qualifying widow(er). (Spouse died of natural causes.)

Exemptions

If more than six imaginary dependents, see page 10.

6a ☐ **Yourself.** If your godfather (or someone else) can claim you as a dependent on his or her return—hey, that's OK, too

  b ☐ **Guard dog**

  c Dependents

    (1) First name _____

        Nickname _____

        Last name _____

    (2) Dependent's relationship to you (e.g., "lousy no-good nephew who should be drowned in a vat of acid before he can squeal to the grand jury again") _____

  d Total number of exemptions claimed _____

  e Total number of exemptions you actually hope to get away with ____

Income

Attach Copy B of your Forms W-2, W-2G, and 1099-R here, along with any gambling IOUs you have a reasonable chance of collecting on.

If you did not get a W-2, see page 12.

If you want us to think you didn't get a W-2, see page 13.

If you got a W-2 from a fictitious construction company, see page 14.

If your W-2 is illegible due to liquor, blood or other stains, see page 15.

Enclose but do not attach any payment.

Note: *Casino chips are not U.S. currency.*

7 Wages, salaries, horse racing tips, etc. Attach Form(s) W-2 _____

8 Loan-shark interest _____

9 Alimony check returned uncashed due to sudden accidental death of ex-spouse _____

10 Total goodwill distributions to the IRA _____

11 Cannabis-farm income or (loss). Attach Schedule F _____

12 Other income. List type, amount, and federal statute broken _____

13 Add the amounts in the far right column for lines 7 through 12. This is your **total income** _____

Adjusted Gross Income

14 Moving expenses _____

Note: *Transporting bodies or body parts across state lines is an itemized deduction, not a moving expense. Use Schedule A*

15 Health insurance deduction. Include any protection money paid here _____

16 Add lines 14 and 15 _____

17 Subtract line 16 from line 13. This is your **adjusted gross income** _____

Tax Computation

If you want the IRS to figure your tax, see page 18.

If you want the IRS to figure your jail sentence, see page 19.

18 Check if: ☐ You were 65 or older ☐ Blind ☐ Honest I didn't see anything Dominick I swear oh God please don't shoot no no no no no. Add the number of boxes checked above and enter the total here _____

19 Subtract line 18 from line 17 _____

20 If line 19 is $30,900 or less, go back to Mr. Alonzo in Queens, grab him by the ankles and shake him upside down vigorously until more loose change falls from his pockets

21 **Taxable income.** Subtract line 20 from line 19 _____

22 Tax

Credits

Multiply $2000 by total number of years you spent on Rikers Island. _____

Other Taxes

23 Alternative under-the-counter minimum tax. Attach bribe to Form 6251 _____

24 Social security and Medicare tax on tip income not reported to employer. Attach Form 4137 _____

25 Subtract Medicare payments for injuries inflicted by employer upon learning about unreported income _____

26 Add lines 23 through 25. This is your **total tax** _____

Payments

27 Federal income tax withheld _____

28 Estimated payments to circuit court judge _____

29 Payment of excessive interest to Vinny _____

30 Add lines 27, 28, and 29. This is your **total payment** _____

Refund

Don't even think about it.

Amount You Owe

That's more like it.

31 If line 26 is more than line 30, subtract line 30 from line 26. This
is the **AMOUNT YOU OWE.** _____

For details on how to pay, be at the Rt. 73 overpass next Tuesday at
midnight.

Sign Here

Do not under any circumstances keep a copy of this return, and better
make sure Ricardo doesn't have one, either.

Under penalty of perjury, I hereby invoke my constitutional privilege
not to incriminate myself.

Your signature _____

Date _____

Your cover occupation _____

Paid Informer's Use Only

Informer's signature _____

Date _____

Next of kin _____

PERSONAL

He twitched awake when the phone rang the first time. His eyelids fluttered like pink hummingbirds and he sat up straight in the chair as if someone might be watching.

"Ding dong the witch is dead," he said stupidly. Then he remembered. He let it ring twice more before picking it up. The voice that answered was new to him, but he knew who it was all right. He had been waiting for her call.

"Hello, Ray? Ray Cain?" If he hadn't just woken up, that voice would've done the job. She sounded like nails across a blackboard.

"No one else would own up to a name like that," he said. "Is this the good witch or the bad witch?"

"Not any kind of witch, silly. This is Angelina Divinidad, remember? You answered my ad at Lovetown.com."

Guilty as charged. He held the printout in his other hand and scanned it carefully, trying to match the woman in the ad with the voice in his ear. No luck. Maybe she had a cold, he thought. Suddenly there was a weird howling noise at her end, and then a slap sounded, and the howling ended abruptly with a strangled sort of yelp.

"What the hell was that?"

"Oh, nothing, honey. Say, are we going to get together or what?"

"You like coffee?"

"Only if I make it myself."

He wasn't expecting that. "So it's your place, then?"

"Sure, why not?"

Why not indeed? "All I need is an address," he said. She gave him one not far from his and he wrote it on the back of a dollar bill. He told her to be all dolled up in about an hour.

"Well, the apartment is a mess..."

"I don't have a date with your apartment," he said, and she tittered nervously. It occurred to him that she laughed exactly the way Stan Laurel used to cry. After he had hung up, he read the ad again.

Wanted: a gentleman and a scholar—and a lover. Must know how to treat a lady, and how to please a woman. Who am I? A big city girl, sometimes, who never wants the night to end. Other times I'm a lost little girl without a friend in the world. Moody. Impetuous. I like to read, to laugh and love. Music makes me sing and dance, and sometimes cry. Beethoven. Someday my prince will come. He could look like you. He could even look like a frog, as long as he's a prince on the inside. I feel I know him already. He loves animals and children and walking in the rain.

He doesn't drink or smoke dope. He is kind and generous, all heart and all man—but not afraid to let the little boy peek out from inside him once in a while. When he peeks at me, he will see a princess.

Beneath the ad was a blank email form where a prince could write the princess in care of Lovetown.com. He had done so out of loneliness and boredom, composing a reply that rivaled her ad for sheer asininity. It embarrassed him to read over the printout now, dripping with phrases like "I enjoy Bach, the Beatles and Benny Goodman, though not necessarily in that order," and "Trees are beautiful too, like old people with stories to tell."

He had hoped she would go for it, but now that she had he was worried. What if her tastes were more educated than his?

What if she were better read? He couldn't tell much from her ad, any more than she could from his email, yet there was something there. She seemed to have a good heart, anyway, and he had never known anyone who truly loved reading and animals to be a complete idiot. It was worth taking a chance on.

He shaved for the first time in weeks, nicking himself in a number of spots and inflicting a bad cut in one. Stanching the flow of blood with a piece of toilet paper, he dusted off a blazer that had hung in his closet for several months and slipped into it. The transformation was immediate. He liked the person in the mirror. He figured just about any woman would go crazy over a face like that—a face full of secret hurt, secret strength. Nothing like a frog, he decided. Every inch a prince. No, he thought, make that a king. Ray Cain, king of the world.

He was almost to her building when an inspiration hit him. Jogging back a few blocks, he stopped at a convenience store and quickly selected a heart-shaped box of candy tied with a red ribbon.

"If you were a girl, wouldn't you like to get candy?" he asked the man behind the counter.

The clerk knotted his brows and fixed him with a look that told him where the door was. The look followed him out the door. A sudden downpour had started while he was inside, and by the time he reached her neighborhood again he was soaked all the way through. He shivered as he pushed the buzzer. Slowly the door opened on a rather dim room that smelled faintly of— diapers? He stepped inside.

"Come on, let's have a look at you," said a voice identical to the one on the phone, only sharper, more piercing. Before his eyes could adjust to the dark, he was literally up to his neck in dogs. One was sniffing him where he didn't care to be sniffed, while the other tried to unbutton his shirt with its teeth. Together they made a howling racket that sounded very familiar.

"Cur! Mudgeon! Get down this instant, you hear me?" He was about to ask if she had attended the Rocky Balboa School of Pet Names when two powerful arms whipped out in unison and smacked each dog on the snout. The arms were attached to a body that would have looked more at home in a vat of formaldehyde. "Hi, I'm Angelina. You must be Ray." He nodded in stunned disbelief and shook her hand. Rough black fur ran up each knuckle. He shuddered. "Won't you sit down? I'll put these two away." Lifting the dogs by their collars until they gagged, she clomped into an adjoining room and dropped or threw them on the floor, where they scrabbled away, yowling.

She clomped back and stood before him. He had never seen anything quite like her. Her skin was the color of paraffin, translucent as a wriggling grub and swollen with hundreds of greenish-blue veins swimming near the surface. She possessed no visible neck. Her head was simply embedded in her torso, and swiveled there like a gigantic, unholy ball bearing. The whites of her eyes swiveled in sockets deep in the whiteness of her skull. Her hair had long ago been bleached of any human color, and hung now to her shoulders in ropy sheets of yellow.

"What have you got there?" she asked coyly. There was hunger in her voice, and behind the hunger, something vaguely ominous. He surrendered the package meekly and she tore it open with a speed that alarmed him. "Ooh! Sweeties!" He wondered numbly if her arms were longer than her legs, and if that would be an evolutionary advantage in an arboreal existence. "I shouldn't, I really shouldn't," she kept saying as she popped piece after piece into her mouth. He was mentally trying to guess her weight when she burst out with a screech and backed away. "Ooh! What happened to your face?"

He drew a hand up to his chin and felt the last trickles of rainwater between his fingers. His face was sticky on the side where he had cut himself. The rain had made the blood run freely.

"A couple of guys tried to get rough," he said. "Luckily, I learned a little judo in the Navy."

"Ooh!" she said, dropping the now-empty box.

"I'll bet you own a thesaurus," he joked out loud.

"No," she replied seriously, "but I've got a jade plant."

There weren't any books around, he noticed. "You just move in?"

"No," she said, puzzled. "I've lived here nearly all my life."

"But your books—?"

"Books?" The word was strange on her tongue. "I don't have any. I mostly read my magazines." He glanced around the room. Recent issues of *People* and *Us Weekly* peered at him from a coffee table. A woman on the cover of *Cosmopolitan* was holding her own breasts and promising to explain "Why Self-Love Is Better Than HIS Love." One corner of the room held a huge boom box and two tiny speakers.

"Is that for Beethoven?" He pointed at the stereo.

"Ooh! Yeah!" she said. She trudged like a bipedal mammoth to a stack of CDs, and dug through it until she found what she wanted. She put it on full volume. It was a mediocre but passable recording of the Fifth, or so he thought until a mechanical drumbeat and an electric bass intruded, and the rhythm changed to disco. Good Lord, could it be? He examined the CD cover. It was. Walter Murphy and the Big Apple Band doing their one and only hit from the *Saturday Night Fever* soundtrack.

Angelina began to dance. She swung with morbid sweeping gestures that would have been perfectly apropos under a full moon and the great pagan columns of Stonehenge. In her little living room they were horrifying. As she swayed like a statue in a hurricane, she brought a cigarette to her lips with one hand and lit it with the other. She closed her eyes dreamily and puffed away. He started to cough.

"I thought you didn't like smoke," he said.

"No, *dope*. I don't like dope. I don't know what I'd do without my ciggies." There was a ceramic reproduction of a man, a cartoon character, on the coffee table. The man had his arms spread wide apart above a caption that read: "I Love You THIS Much." Ray hefted the figurine in his palms and gazed meditatively at the top of Angelina's head. I always was a coward, he thought with genuine regret. He set the figurine back down on the table and escaped quietly through the front door while Angelina's eyes were closed in religious ecstasy. As soon as he was around the corner he ran and didn't stop until he was back in his apartment. He locked the door, turned off the lights and pulled the shades.

When the phone rang a few minutes later, he put it on vibrate and held it gently against his aching forehead.

Your Falling Stars

CANCER (June 21 – July 22)

Stop worrying. Just because you *are* a Cancer doesn't mean you *have* cancer. Not necessarily. Heart disease is the number one killer, not cancer. Cancer is only number two. A big number two, but still nowhere near as popular as your workaday heart attack. The chances are that you'll have a cardiac arrest on your wedding night before your liver ever turns black and swells up like a malignant watermelon. Don't think about it. You don't have it. Or do you? God, what if you did and you never knew until it was too late? You have been coughing an awful lot lately. And that sore hasn't healed yet. Was that tiny lump always there, or...? Oh, don't be silly. It's probably benign, whatever it is. Don't think about it. They say thinking about it makes it happen. So don't think about it.

LEO (July 23 – August 22)

Count your blessings—you never know when one might be missing! But seriously, just be thankful you aren't prone to cancer, like some signs. At least you have a fighting chance.

VIRGO (August 23 – September 22)

Death is something we all have to face sooner or later. To some—the lucky ones—it comes quickly, quietly, even beautifully. Say, in a heart attack. To others it is an insidious lingering illness, a mysterious and unrelenting assailant, a terminal horror. The Greeks had a word for it. They called it cancer. But what the hell did the Greeks know? They drank hemlock for kicks. They liked little boys. Where do they get off talking about your cancer? Wait a minute—you say you're a *Virgo*? I thought you were a *Cancer*! I'm sorry. I was looking at someone else's chart. You don't have cancer at all. You'll live to be 150. Probably die in a train wreck. I didn't mean to frighten you. My mistake. Won't happen again.

LIBRA (September 23 – October 23)

You will probably get up today. If not, you are already dead. What are you reading this for? Go on, get out of here. You bother me. And take your cancer with you.

SCORPIO (October 24 – November 22)

Never say never. No matter how bleak things look, there's always hope. Every year they spend millions of dollars on research. They kill thousands of innocent laboratory rats trying to save one person like you. Eventually they'll find a cure. They've got to. It simply can't go on like this, year after year, people dropping like flies, helpless against the enemy within. It's madness. It's got to stop, that's all. Don't give up. If you were a Cancer, I'd say give up. But you're not. Hang in there, old buddy.

SAGITTARIUS *(November 23 – December 21)*

You will see something today you have seen before. Copper is the chief mineral export of Chile. Titan is one of the moons of Saturn. Cancer is "a malignant tumor of potentially unlimited growth that expands locally by invasion and systematically by metastasis." Good luck.

CAPRICORN *(December 22 – January 19)*

You are "any of various hollow-horned ruminant mammals (esp. of the genus *Capra*) related to the sheep but of lighter build and with backwardly arching horns, a short tail, and usually straight hair." It could be worse, right? You could have cancer. Maybe you do. Just kidding!

AQUARIUS *(January 20 – February 19)*

Oh God, help me. Please. The doctors say it won't be long now. All they can do is ease some of the pain. Why me, God? Why me? I raised two beautiful kids and slaved to buy a house for *this*? What did I do wrong? Sure, I used to smoke two packs a day. Now I can't even lift one little cigar to my lips. People would ask me nicely to stop and I'd just blow smoke rings in their faces. "Everything causes cancer these days," I told them. "When your time is up, you're gonna go." I was joking, Lord. You know that. I didn't know it would be like this. Not so soon. Help me. Please.

PISCES (February 20 – March 20)

You're being hysterical. The actual release of radiation at Fukushima was minimal. The public was never in real danger at any time. The world needs nuclear power. There are risks involved in everything. You are more likely to develop cancer by standing in the sun than you are by standing next to a nuclear power plant. Next question.

ARIES (March 21 – April 19)

What would you rather have—a few pesticide residues, or billions of bugs all over everything? There's no proof any of that stuff causes cancer. Anyway, you're only talking about a couple of migrant farm workers and a few California Condors already on the way out.

TAURUS (April 20 – May 20)

"We are all under sentence of death." Kafka said that. And look at him today. If he were alive, he'd probably have cancer.

GEMINI (May 21 – June 20)

It is later than you think.

CALL ME SPARKLES

It is long past time for me to come out. For far too long—my whole life, in fact—I have lived with a painful (and what I mistakenly believed was a shameful) secret: I am a unicorn living in a man's body.

There. I've said it. What relief those few simple words give me!

True, I didn't have a unicorn mother or father. Both of my parents were human, kind of, even though one was a Young Republican. I don't have a single distinctive unicorn gene in my physiological makeup, except in the sense that the human genome has always shared a general 96 percent overlap with the unicorn genome. I do not in any obvious way resemble a unicorn. Not yet, anyway. But now I have come to understand that being a unicorn is more than a question of mere DNA, more than a matter of outward appearances. It is not something that can be verified or falsified with a laboratory test. It is at least partly a social construct. In the end, it is largely a matter of how each individual identifies.

I identify as a unicorn. I always have. When I was five years old I started signing my name Starlite (that's Rainbow Brite's unicorn to the uninitiated), until my parents beat me and sent me to my room without any oats. Now, at last, I am ready to accept my true nature, with both pride and humility. Pride, because frankly it takes some balls— albeit not large, furry unicorn balls—to own who you are, especially when that admission comes with so much prejudice and societal baggage. And humility because, well, unicorns! They are so awesome, so beautiful. I cry whenever I think of them. I'm crying now, gently, with soft, neighing, unicorn-like sobs.

So you see, though I was not technically born a unicorn, I sort of was, actually. There are some who claim that being a unicorn is a choice. They are wrong. Not evil, perhaps (except for that awful God-Hates-Unicorns church), simply wrong. You cannot choose who or what you are. You can only choose whether or not to accept it. Which brings me to my next point.

This news may not be welcomed or even understood by all of my family and friends. My ex-girlfriend and children naturally see me differently—my ex as a "vile bug who somehow escaped the killing jar," and my children as a loving caregiver and mentor. Will they be able to see me as a unicorn, even if unicorns are so rare that nobody has ever quite managed to see one? Will they still love me? I mean of course my children, not my ex, who has already put out three hits on me, and will probably just hire a couple of unicorn hunters to take me out when she hears this.

Those hunters will not have much trouble finding me. By making this public announcement I have put a gigantic target on myself. Anyone can take a shot at me, and no doubt many will, even if only rhetorically. I will be even easier to locate when I complete the physical part of my transformation. Years ago, when I first formulated this plan, I secretly began taking unicorn hormones, which for some reason are not extracted from unicorns but rather from readers of Japanese manga. Now you know how the paparazzi got those embarrassing shots of me snorting like a racehorse, pawing the ground and occasionally leaping over rainbows.

Soon I will approach even closer to my ideal when I have thousands of specks of glitter permanently embedded in my flesh, my DNA is altered to allow me to grow soft white fur over my entire body, and I have a long, pointed white horn surgically attached to my forehead. Regardless of where my changes take me, however, the important thing is that I am ready now, finally, to be myself, the real me.

In celebration of this joyful day I say to you now, don't call me Kurt any longer. Call me Sparkles! And while you're here, could you fetch me that feedbag full of oats?

THE WIMPOSIUM: A SOCRATIC DIALOGUE

Persons of the Dialogue

SOCRATES, A Greek philosopher and timeshare salesman

HERPES, A slave

BIKEATHON, A Spartan athlete

MEDIOCRATES, An affluent used chariot dealer

Scene: A public bathhouse in Athens, Greece

MEDIOCRATES: Lower, a little lower... Ah, yes, 'tis good. But I pray you, Bikeathon, do be gentle with that towel. My extremities were sorely chafed in the games.

BIKEATHON: *(Dropping the towel in anger)* Dry yourself, then, by Zeus! A fine Spartan you would make, whining and whimpering till the very gods are sick of it.

(Enter Socrates. The bath attendant checks his tunic at the desk, and then he joins his comrades in the steam room.)

SOCRATES: Whatever can you mean, good Bikeathon? How can Mediocrates be a Spartan when already he is a citizen of Athens?

BIKEATHON: Oh piss off, Socrates.

MEDIOCRATES: Yes, we're in no mood for your games today.

SOCRATES: Let us look into the truth of the matter.

BIKEATHON: Let us not and say we did.

SOCRATES: By "Spartan," do you refer to a native or inhabitant of Sparta, or merely to someone who has his mail forwarded there? Or perhaps to one who has a cousin who knows of a woman whose father, it is rumored, once sent a servant on an errand there, and did not pay him? Or are you speaking rather of an ideal "Spartanness" of which all things Spartan-like must be composed in order to retain their essential Spartanhood, that is to say, their Spartaneity?

BIKEATHON: *(Kneeing Socrates in the groin)* Does this clarify my position, Athenian dog? *(Socrates doubles over in agony)*

MEDIOCRATES: That was beautiful, Bikeathon. Do it again.

BIKEATHON: With pleasure. Eat a boot, Socrates! *(Kicks him savagely)*

SOCRATES: *(Gasping for breath)* Your comment perplexes me, Mediocrates. How can you discourse of the beautiful without first inquiring into beauty itself, or that which partakes of beauteousness—your serving boy, for example?

MEDIOCRATES: Yon Herpes?

SOCRATES: The very same.

MEDIOCRATES: He is yours for a thousand drachmas.

SOCRATES: Done. But first I would speak with the lad and define the terms of my argument. He is of lowly birth and simpleminded, no doubt, but perhaps he has a taste for true philosophy.

BIKEATHON: Bah! True buggery, you mean.

MEDIOCRATES: Herpes! Come hither. Socrates would question you.

HERPES: Yes?

SOCRATES: Boy, if your tunic were to fall off in the forest and there were no one but myself to hear it, truly, could it be said never to have happened?

HERPES: Very truly.

SOCRATES: And if I then ordered you to don womanish attire while I disciplined you with hot olive branches, would that, too, be a matter of the intellect only, and of no interest to the authorities?

HERPES: Indeed.

SOCRATES: Most excellent. I have but one other question: What is that strange and horrible goblin standing behind you?

HERPES: *(Turning quickly)* Where?

SOCRATES: There! *(Knocks him out with a small marble statuette)* Thank you, Mediocrates. He is a quick-witted youth after all, but not quick enough. Again I am in your debt. *(Starts to drag Herpes off)*

MEDIOCRATES: Not so fast, Socrates. Have you forgotten the thousand drachmas?

SOCRATES: Er, no. That is, could you wait until Friday, so to speak?

MEDIOCRATES: The Delphic oracle has said, "He who welches must soak his dentures in the river Styx." Bikeathon, submerge our learned friend in the healing waters.

BIKEATHON: Gladly. *(Dunks Socrates in the bath)* Drink from the Fountain of Truth, learned sponge!

SOCRATES: *(Gurgling)* But what is truth?

BIKEATHON: Tell me and we will both know; that is, we shall know that we know, and in knowing, know that the knowable is known to those in the know—know what I mean?

SOCRATES: Styx and stones may break my bones, but... Glug, glug, glug! *(He disappears)*

BIKEATHON: Very true.

MEDIOCRATES: Indeed.

DREAM ON

"What a piece of work is a man!" said Shakespeare; and while it's possible he was merely gazing into the mirror and feeling his own biceps, he was probably referring to the human mind. A mysterious thing, the mind. One man discovers the principle of electromagnetic anti-gravitational polarity, and wins a Nobel Prize. Another one owns and operates a Kentucky Fried Chicken franchise. Perhaps it is the same man wearing a different suit, but in that case he is moonlighting and should declare his second source of income (the Nobel Committee).

The point is, few students of the mind have any inkling of its innermost workings, particularly at the subconscious, or street level. One who did during the first half of the 20th century was Dr. Aloysius Gilbert, dream researcher and founder of the Gilbert Institute for Advanced and Gruesome Studies, which has given hope to so many. Dr. Gilbert was originally a follower of Freud, till one day Freud noticed he was being followed, and spun around suddenly to confront him.

"Just what are you looking at, eh?"

"The back of your head," replied Gilbert, with the candor that was his genius. Freud was so moved by his frankness that he immediately rubbed out a lit cigar on the young man's bald spot. The two became fast friends, remaining inseparable throughout the next 30 minutes, until they broke intellectually over who would pay for the cigar. Afterward, Ghastly credited Freud with teaching him "everything there is to know about eczema, and then some," and how to get big laughs at parties by impersonating a lemur.

He soon had a flourishing psychoanalytic practice in Vienna—one so lucrative, in fact, that his wife Grimelda could never comprehend why he persisted in renting himself out as a cuspidor on weekends (poverty had been his close companion during childhood, although when the two met later at a class reunion they hardly recognized each other).

But in treating thousands of refried psyches he sometimes resorted to methods that were, like those of Colonel Kurtz, "unsound." One former patient charged that, under hypnosis, he had made her don a little sailor suit to "do the hokey pokey." Worse, none of the respectable journals would publish his papers on dreams, forcing him to send his feverish theories to the only outlet open to him, *Scatology Today*, where the following cases and comments by Dr. Gilbert first appeared. These are the pivotal works which, in their collective unconsciousness and their intuitive grasp of dream symbology, Carl Jung declared "every bit as profound as the lyrics to 'Row, Row, Row Your Boat.' "

Case of Anna S.

My new patient, a typical bourgeoise, will not lie down on the couch without first compulsively sweeping it clean of imaginary insects. Even then I have to sit on her chest to keep her there. All this because one little silverfish happened to explore her underthings at our initial session. Will I never understand the id? This morning she related an important dream:

"I am in my apartment, which is the same as usual except that it has been repainted a cheerful shade of black and a new wing has been added to accommodate the wax museum exhibit of my family. A surprise party is being thrown in my honor, and I am delighted to no end until I realize I was not invited. Suddenly depressed, I sit down on a miniature schnauzer I used to play with as a child, and begin to weep. But the dog accuses me of being a sentimentalist and of putting on weight besides. I become suicidal, and am just about to end it all by eating my mother's cooking when my own voice, coming from the clock radio, announces that I have won the Joseph Goebbels Look-alike Contest. Overcome with joy, I awake and slit my wrists."

What a lucid expression of wish fulfillment! Clearly, Anna S. is less concerned with the normal childhood traumas than with the fact that she was never given a last name, and has had to make do all her life with a middle initial. Even becoming a high-ranking Nazi would be preferable, though it would require a complete change of wardrobe. When I pointed this out to her she seemed very grateful and kissed my hand, then bit down as hard as she could on my ring finger, an obvious display of jealousy which nearly caused me to achieve escape velocity.

Case of Ernst A.

This afternoon as I was mopping up my office (with my receptionist) I spotted a small boy fondling the cushions on the couch. After cuffing him soundly, I asked him how it was possible for a child his age to grow a full-length Vandyke. He explained that he was not a child at all but an adult whose growth had been stunted by guilt, and that the couch had reminded him of his mother.

"Oh? And when did you last have your mother reupholstered?" I asked.

"Only yesterday," he replied. I knew he had come to me in the nick of time. In a fearful sweat, he told me his recurring nightmare:

"I am strolling alongside the Danube admiring the view and trying to work up enough courage to throw myself in, when I see a beautiful rainbow arching over the river and ending somewhere in the Vienna Woods. Suddenly I am in the heart of the forest, and it occurs to me that I have forgotten to bring any insect repellent. This strikes me as very funny at the time, but when I try to laugh the only thing that emerges from my lips is a tiny flag reading 'Ha ha.' I become alarmed, and decide to hide under an oak leaf until spring comes. Before I can touch it, the leaf turns into a leprechaun standing by a pot of gold. The leprechaun confides that he is merely waiting for the gold market to hit a new high before he liquidates his assets, but that if I give him the magic acorn I can have the whole pot for practically nothing. Just as I am about to ask, 'What acorn?' he disappears, and I wake up under the bed." He sighed as he concluded his story.

"Where, exactly, did you say this pot of gold could be found?"

"Nowhere," he answered, pretending to look confused. "It was just a dream."

"Don't play games," I warned, backing him against the wall.

"No, please!" he begged as he tried to edge out the door. He was about to run for it when I snatched him up by the scruff of the neck and thrashed him back into his dream world. Then I lifted the magic acorn from his shirt pocket, loaded my Luger, and went for a walk in the Vienna Woods.

LAKE DELAVAN DAYS

For others, the word "vacation" evokes idyllic childhood memories of family togetherness and carefree summer days spent at some garden spot by a seashore or lake. For me, "vacation" has always meant a special family time, too—a time where families retreat far from civilization for the express purpose of torturing one another in an enclosed space without distractions. It doesn't take a $90-an-hour Freudian to trace this feeling directly back to that fateful Luchs family trip to Lake Delavan, Wisconsin.

The year was 1964. Kennedy was freshly planted in Arlington National Cemetery, having been killed (as Oliver Stone has since informed us) by a conspiracy involving 93 percent of the American people and at least two of Donald Duck's nephews, Huey and Dewey (although there is no direct evidence that Louie helped Oswald pull the trigger, he is now known to have been on a first-name basis with both Jack Ruby and Sirhan Sirhan). The Beatles were continuing their full frontal assault on America's youth. Vietnam was becoming the number one vacation spot for draft-age U.S. males.

The Luchses had just purchased a peculiar little foreign car, a Citroën 2CV. This vehicle is several sizes larger than a Tonka Toy and almost as powerful. It's basically a Volkswagen Bug with an inferiority complex and only two cylinders. The man who sold it to us—a family friend later convicted of extortion and threatening to set off a bomb in the San Francisco Hilton, but that's another story—fondly described the 2CV as "the perfect desert fighting machine." He claimed that if you ran out of motor oil, you could always keep a Citroën going by filling the crankcase with ripe bananas. More than once our father caught us attempting to put this intriguing theory to the test.

The 2CV could seat two comfortably. In a pinch, four people could be squeezed in if they were willing to forego minor comforts like breathing. Our car held all nine of us: our parents, Robert and Jeannine, and (in descending order of age and location in the food chain), Hilde, Kurt, Murph, Helmut, Sarah, Rolf and Cara. Then there was our "luggage" (paper bags full of old clothes), the inflatable rubber boat, life preservers, a week's worth of food and two cats, Leopold and Loeb.

The main excitement on the trip up came when one of the cats leapt from the back seat onto Dad's back as he was negotiating a left turn. He screamed, "Get it off, get it off!" but this only amused his passengers and caused the cat to dig in its claws, piercing his Goldwater T-shirt and drawing enough blood to simulate a lovely tie-dyed effect. The rest of the ride is a blur to me now, since I spent most of it vomiting into a bag of Hilde's knitting. Like most healthy American families, ours included both normal vomiters (NVs) and projectile vomiters (PVs). The difference is, if an NV keeps his head in a paper bag most of the time, his fellow travelers will only enjoy his experience vicariously, whereas there is no escape from the PV. Handing a PV a paper bag is like putting a cherry bomb in a coffee can: It simply makes for a messier explosion. I was an NV, but Sarah was a PV, and by the time we reached Delavan the interior of the car looked like a gutted animal.

On first sight Lake Delavan appeared to be North America's largest mud puddle. At no point could you see bottom. Yet it was so shallow you could wade out for a quarter of a mile and never get your head wet. Not that you really wanted to get your head wet in Lake Delavan. It seemed to have become the final resting place for all the sewage, crumpled gum wrappers, rusty beer cans and broken glass in the tri-state area. Dull, sticky soap bubbles covered everything, bubbles that emitted a sickening stench when popped.

The cabin was owned by an old Polish woman from Chicago and was apparently furnished with cast-offs from the Warsaw ghetto. Before the electricity was turned on we wandered from room to room, weeping like icons at the shabbiness of it all. "What's that crunching noise?" asked Rolf. "Sounds like Rice Krispies," said Hilde. When the lights came on we discovered that the cabin was carpeted with dead flies. Helmut got Sarah to eat one by convincing her she would magically acquire the power of flight. She was indeed airborne for several seconds after jumping from the cabin roof, but problems with low visibility and faulty hydraulics forced her to make an emergency landing in some sumac bushes.

The only water sport we encountered at Lake Delavan was trying to get the toilet to flush. We quickly ascertained that any amount of toilet paper, even a single square, would cause an overflow. This more than anything else drove us away. Although we had paid for the entire week, by Thursday we had all had enough. We packed up and left late that afternoon with Dad even more dazed and confused than usual.

Dad was always in a world of his own, and never more so than when he was driving. He was very superstitious. He thought it was bad luck to look at a map before a trip...or during a trip...or at any time, for that matter. He also believed it was poor form to accost strangers with questions like, "Where the hell are we?" And he nursed an instinctive fear of policemen bordering on divine awe. (There must be genes for all these traits, because I regret to say they were passed on to me!)

Unfortunately, when the 2CV was fully locked and loaded with Luchses it was unable to exceed 35 miles per hour, 10 miles below the minimum. A state trooper (who probably thought he had stepped into a remake of *The Grapes of Wrath*) soon pulled us over and advised Dad that he would have to leave the main highway and use back roads with lower speed limits the rest of the way. When we turned off the main road we got lost immediately and stayed lost. Mom held the thankless post of navigator. Her pathetic attempts to read the map by flashlight while in motion so infuriated Dad that he snatched the map away from her, wrapped it around the steering wheel with one hand and turned the flashlight on it with the other. This maneuver caused us to narrowly miss an A&W Root Beer truck.

The afternoon wore into twilight. It began to rain. The winter solstice drew near. I don't remember when—or if—we ever got home, and I don't want to remember. And I'll thank you not to mention the word "vacation" again.

One High Fever, Unabridged

I'm no Dale Carnegie, God knows, but I recently stumbled upon a principle of mental health that no person wishing to retain his sanity should ignore. In short, it is this: Never open a dictionary unless you have a specific word, a particular verbal destination in mind. To do otherwise is to play Russian roulette with your faculties, the difference being that with a dictionary there is, so to speak, a bullet in every chamber. I speak from bitter, brutal experience.

Just this morning I was searching Random House's dictionary for *clupeid*, that is, "kloo' pe id, n., any of the *Clupeidae*, a family of chiefly marine, teleostean fishes, including the herrings, sardines, menhaden and shad." I read through that definition 19 times. It had a rhythm as compelling as any by Bob Marley and the Wailers. By the time "clupeid" had burned pinholes in my pupils, I had forgotten why I had looked the word up in the first place. Luck had been on my side, though. I had set out to locate a single word and had done so without bringing shame to myself or my family (a family of chiefly marine, teleostean fishes, by the way). I had been able, after some effort, to avert my gaze to an especially informative advertisement for women's undergarments in a nearby mail-order catalog belonging to my girlfriend. Where was she now, the traitor? Shopping, probably; leaving me here alone with the *Random House Unabridged*. As well to leave a child in the same room with a man named Guido.

I opened the volume and quite by chance stood goggling at the same page where, in my innocent youth, I had looked up "clupeid." The hair at the back of my neck slowly stiffened with re-pulsion. I had landed full force on *clypeus* (klip' e es), "the area of the facial wall of an insect's head between the labrum and the frons, usually separated from the latter by a groove." Think of that! On the facial wall of every last verminous bug in the world, the clypeus was separated from the frons by a mere groove! Who could bear it? I ran a trembling index finger down the column, hoping for a soothing adjective, a prosaic noun to calm my nerves.

Instead, the final word on the page transfixed me: *Cnidocyst* (ni' de sist). It had a foul, almost sinister sound. I repeated it several times in spite of myself. Cnidocyst. *Cnidocyst.* What it was I didn't know, and I didn't want to know. But it was too late for squeamishness. I read on.

Why, a cnidocyst was nothing but a nematocyst! It said so right there in black and white. How foolish I had been after all. And a nematocyst was... well, a nematocyst was simply a... a... what was it, anyway? According to the ghouls at Random House, a nematocyst is "an organ in coelenterates consisting of a minute capsule containing a thread capable of being ejected and causing a sting, used for protection and for capturing prey."

A more flimsy tissue of euphemisms would be impossible to concoct. "Capable of being ejected," the man says. I'd like to see the one that *isn't* ejected! "Used for protection and for capturing prey." Indeed. It's used for making a damn nuisance, if I know my coelenterates—and I think I do. If I had a nematocyst to my name those coelenterates wouldn't be swaggering like psychotic sailors, capturing helpless prey and causing wholesale carnage, no sir. There wouldn't be a coelenterate standing in the joint when I finished with them. I could lick 'em all, I could—I checked myself before complete hysteria had hold of me.

I was beginning to wish I had stayed with "cnidocyst." Innuendo was preferable to outright horror. I felt a compulsion to turn back to "cnidocyst," praying that the sight of a familiar word, however nauseating, would take my mind off the chilling implications of "nematocyst." Any port in a storm. On the way to "cnidocyst" I paused among the "D's" long enough to pick up another happy zoological term, "dulosis," or "the enslavement of an ant colony or its members by ants of a different species." Slavery, right here in modern North America! What next?

I made it back to "cnidocyst" all right, but there was little relief in the reunion. It sounded as ugly as ever, and if a cnidocyst was a nematocyst and vice versa, any preference of mine amounted to a choice of evils, no more. Lost in thought, I let my gaze wander. I gaped at the word above "cnidocyst." It was "cnidocil," obviously a close relative. There was the same squinty, pinch-faced look, the same unctuous air of authority. *Cnidocil* (ni' de sil), "a hairlike sensory process projecting from the surface of a cnidoblast, believed to trigger the discharge of the nematocyst."

"A hairlike sensory process"—again, the words were vague but the images they conjured up were not. I had the desperate certainty that if I encountered a hairlike sensory process, even a small one, I would be incapable of any reaction except screaming myself into a dead faint.

I noted the stock journalistic jargon, "*believed* to trigger the discharge of the nematocyst" (my italics). It's considered poor form among journalists, and I suppose, by extension, among the compilers of dictionaries, to prejudice a case by making direct accusations against any of the parties involved, even when their guilt is a public fact. Thus we have "suspected" assassins, "confessed" kidnappers, and cnidocils "believed" to trigger the discharge of the nematocyst.

But in analyzing this nicety I was forgetting a very important factor, the word just above "cnidocil"—"cnidoblast," or in plain Pig Latin, "the cell within which a nematocyst is developed." Clearly I had situated myself within a massive web of intrigue, a conspiracy of international proportions. The cnidocil was a triggerman, a gunsel working for the cnidoblast, who was shielding the nematocyst, alias the cnidocyst, alias the "cnida" (from the Greek word for nettle). Paranoid psychosis nearly had me in its grip. I was sinking fast. I fought to maintain consciousness as I babbled like Gertrude Stein, "A cnidocyst is a nematocyst is a cnida is a nematocyst is a—" Then, mercifully, I passed out.

The touch of a cold, wet cloth on my forehead brought me to. I recoiled at first, then allowed my face to be stroked by a pair of delicate feminine hands. It was my girlfriend, back from her shopping spree.

"I told you never to drink before sunset," she chided me. "You never listen, do you?"

"Easy, hon, or I'll sic my nematocyst on you," I said.

"What were you drinking—alcohol or chloroform? Come on now, get your head up. Let me show you what I found at the mall: a brand new hair extension!"

"You mean a hairlike sensory process," I said. She let my head fall back onto the tile and went to mix herself a double Scotch and soda, no ice.

UFO's: The Secret Air Force Files

Through a top-level security leak at the Pentagon, we were able to gain access to the most guarded information in the world, the Air Force's file on unidentified flying objects. Up until now these reports were known only to the Russians and the Chinese, and then only in very poor translations. At last the truth can be told.

❊ ❊ ❊ ❊ ❊

INCIDENT: March 17, 1962. Three giant cigar-shaped objects were sighted over New York City, flying in formation with a huge ashtray. Millions of seemingly normal citizens witnessed one of the objects blow a definite smoke ring over Manhattan and then flick some ashes on Brooklyn. Then, within seconds the entire formation had lifted away, signaled a left turn and vanished, never to be seen again.

EXPLANATION: In this case the *observers* are fictional, not the UFOs. It is common knowledge that there are no actual human beings living in New York. The humanoid apparitions you see on the streets and in office buildings are optical illusions caused by the action of the sun's rays on blacktop. If you blink, they will disappear.

❊ ❊ ❊ ❊ ❊

INCIDENT: On Thursday, December 14, 1989, Enoch Waffler, a beet farmer in Spastic Colon, North Dakota, had this experience:

"I was walking along this here furrow, planting beet seeds with a rivet gun, when this big sorta flying bedpan whizzes by at 100,000 miles per hour, shooting sparks and making a noise like a coon hound with its tail caught in a door. I know it was 100,000 miles per hour because 15 minutes later he had circled the Earth completely and was back at my place asking directions to the Crab Nebula. I say 'he' but I mean it was a little feller—oh, about two or three feet tall in his socks— with eyes like silver dollars and hands like pliers with tiny golden beaks. Well, we got to talking, and I gave him some corn whiskey, which he spit right up again. But he did drink a whole five-gallon can of kerosene. Got mad as a killer bee when I couldn't find him any dry ice. Then he was off again, looking for a gas station that stayed open all night and sold pluto-nium. But first he posed for some snapshots and I got the whole thing on a recorder which I talk into while planting beets, to keep from going crazy."

EXPLANATION: Mr. Waffler was the victim of a well-rehearsed prank. What he thought was an extraterrestrial visitor was most likely a little neighbor boy in a homemade costume. The boy then invented a nuclear-powered starship capable of speeds up to 100,000 miles per hour to complete the hoax. Either that or he stopped the Earth from rotating on its axis so it would *look* as though he were going 100,000 miles per hour. In either case the boy is very clever and should be watched. Waffler should have caught on, though, when the "alien" asked how to get to the Crab Nebula. Everybody knows it's closed on weekdays.

IT'S FUNNY UNTIL SOMEONE LOSES AN EYE (THEN IT'S *Really* FUNNY)

❀ ❀ ❀ ❀ ❀

INCIDENT: Saturday, June 28, 2003, Albert Schmecker, a part-time glue-sniffer, returned to his home in Peoria to find it surrounded by a pulsating mass of airborne lights. He then heard a piercing shriek, and would've run away had he not realized it was his own. He fell to his knees, trembling. An awesome shape loomed out of the unearthly glare. He later described it as "one of those synthesizers with the color charts on the keyboard and the rhythm section that plays by itself." The synthesizer played a medley of old favorites while the lights flickered softly as if in response, and soon Schmecker was lulled into a deep sleep. When he awoke his house was gone, with only a slight indentation in the grass to show where it had once stood.

EXPLANATION: He was behind in the payments.

MISSING: ONE LINK

The search for an ancestor that might link the human to the inhuman goes on, like the search for Jimmy Hoffa (some experts feel that when we have found the one we will have found the other). What did our remote predecessors look like? No one knows, but all the indications are that in a family portrait, you'd want them to be holding the camera.

The hominid fossil record is scant—mostly jaws and teeth—and even this slim evidence was compromised by the recent discovery that these fossils are actually false teeth which the early men took out at bedtime and forgot to put back in. How and why they also took out their jaws is still a mystery.

What we do know about ancient man we have gleaned by picking through his garbage and going over his quarterly financial statements, and by talking to a woman named Maggie who knew him well. Maggie was a charwoman who became a slightly charred woman during the MGM Grand Hotel/Casino fire in Las Vegas in 1980.

"Not only were his teeth false, but his beard, too," she said to us as she beat a still-smoldering Persian rug with a bullwhip. "I met him here in Vegas during Reagan's first presidential campaign, sure. He was a little guy, about five-feet-two, eyes of blue—both on one side of his head, unfortunately. He was old, real old...about two million years, tops. No wonder he always insisted on the senior discount. I think it was him that started the fire. He cried on my shoulder one time and told me he was sore as all get out because he had invented fire way back when and never saw a penny of the royalties."

Maggie paused thoughtfully. "One morning he took the blueberries off his cereal, stomped the juice out of 'em and painted the walls of his room with a dead branch—pictures of bison and ritual sacrifice, you know, but cute, like a little boy would do. He was just like a kid sometimes, always sulking because he knew his cranial capacity was about half the modern average and he couldn't wear a hat without it falling over his ears. Also, he walked like Walter Brennan, but I told him it would never change the way I felt about him—I still hated him."

Did this early man possess a brow only a bit higher than that of a teamster, or did he approach the human norm? Well, I don't want to imply that his skull was pointed, but if you threw him headfirst into a dartboard he'd probably stick.

He used no "tools" as we know them today, although he was apparently able to crack nuts with his forehead and saw down trees with his eyebrow ridges. In short, he closely resembled a Chicago alderman, except that he lacked the power of speech, as did his wife—which is about the only good thing we can say about either of them, bless their hearts.

I Concede

Although the late returns are still coming in, I think it's time to face reality and acknowledge that my opponents have won, and I have lost. There is no shame in losing—except, of course, the shame of losing. But I'm here to tell you that this campaign is about more than winning and losing.

I am comforted by the knowledge that my candidacy provided a lively platform from which to seriously address the pressing issues of the day—issues like, "Who is Kurt Luchs, that the gods should torment him so with low standings in the polls?" Now that my hopes have ended in defeat, it is time to let go of the struggle and simply wish in my heart of hearts that, as it must to all men, death will come to my opponents—a lingering and horribly painful death involving buboes and carbuncles swelling in the groin and armpits. I take comfort in knowing that, while my opponents received 60 percent of the votes cast by independents, I received 100 percent of the votes cast by Kurt Luchs.

There were so many meaningful moments in this campaign, moments I will always treasure. At one rally, a thoughtful voter asked me, "If you could press a button and make your opponents disappear, would you do so?" I didn't like the question, so I pressed a button and my security detail made the man who asked it disappear. On another occasion a hostile reporter asked me if my years of struggle in posh private schools and the halls of privilege had turned me unhealthily inward and made me a solipsist. After looking it up, I can assure each and every one of my imaginary friends that I am not a solipsist. The correct term, I believe, is megalomaniac. And I think it will be a long time before anyone forgets my "I Have a Recurring Dream About Halle Berry and Kate Hudson" speech.

My opponents and I disagree on many issues such as bestiality, Satan worship, and cannibalizing the newborn, but we all agree on the general direction for this country. Other than my continuing activism in the causes I believe in—like a system to carry mail for all Americans—I have no immediate plans personally except to retreat to a quiet place of reflection where I can torture my family in privacy and begin my long, agonizing slide into embittered alcoholism. As Julia Roberts said in *Pretty Woman*, I want the whole fairy tale.

Let me promise you this, my friends: Though I have lost the election, and public interest in my opinions has dwindled to absolute zero, I will continue to snipe from the sidelines, to nip at the heels of my onetime opponents like a rabid schnauzer and to denounce them on Fox News whenever the guards once more permit me in the studio. In short, though I have dropped any pretense of seeking to become a public servant, I will continue to be a public nuisance until my sniveling, miserable opponents give up out of sheer fatigue.

Thank you.

Desserts of the Troglodytes

We continue our survey of foods around the world (see "Strudels of the Outer Mongolian Steppes" and "After-Dinner Mints of the Kalahari Bushmen") with a look at the desserts of the post-apocalyptic troglodytes of Central Wisconsin, a distinct cultural and linguistic group of semi-humans accidentally created in the wake of the total nuclear war initiated by the forty-fifth President of the United States.

Some of our more cynical readers may doubt that the troglodytes *have* any desserts, but I assure you they do, and very fine desserts they are, too. They may not always have time for a seven-course dinner, those troglodytes, but they enjoy their desserts as much as the next man. In fact, there's no surer way to enrage one of these gentle, slightly radioactive nomads than by hiding his dessert. And what antics! First he'll tear his hair out, then in a sudden attack of remorse he'll try to paste it back on with some "bokku" (mud), and then he'll throw his oatmeal on the ground and cry himself to sleep like a baby. It really is something to see, if you have the heart to carry it off.

It may surprise you to learn that these hardy, vanishing people have their cake and eat it too, though it's actually more of a simple mud pie filled with nutritious minerals and other small rocks, and often garnished with flying insects, forget-me-nots and what-have-you's. These plain slices of "kreenod" (mud) need not be cooked. They need not be eaten, either.

Another after-dinner delicacy popular with the troglodytes is "bokku-ninga," or muddy dog (literally, "living hairy filth"). The origins of this dish are obscure, and it's probably just as well. Perhaps it has something to do with the abundance of dogs, and the even greater abundance of mud ("shoobiki") in the area. The problem is how to bring the two together at a temperature high enough to keep the taste buds from growing suspicious.

To catch the dog, there are several common ploys. One way is simply to stand there and yell "Here, Sport!" or "Come and get it, Duke!" at the top of your lungs. This doesn't fool any dog worth eating, but for some reason the canines find it an irresistibly funny line, and it never fails to crack them up. The Central Wisconsin feral dog, after all, has a highly developed sense of humor. He will laugh himself sick, thus becoming an easy prey to troglodytes and other forms of carnivorous plant life. From there it's an easy matter to freeze the dog with dry ice, stuff him with confetti and one shredded Sunday edition of the *New York Times,* and lower him into a vat containing not more than 236 and not less than 235 gallons of hot mud, plus a dash of chives. I can tell you right now, if you don't have the chives it's not worth the trouble; although if you *do* have chives I can't see why you should bother with the dog or, for that matter, with the mud. Cooked muddy dog, by the way, is a dessert admitting of endless variations, and its taste has been described as being anywhere from "a little bit like shoe leather" to "quite a bit like shoe leather."

By this time in the festivities most troglodytes have either passed out or taken to writhing on the ground. Unless my interpreter is kidding, this ritual means "my compliments to the chef,"

"hail to the chief," or words to that effect. For the few rugged individuals left standing, however, there is one final concoction,
the *crème de la crème* of post-apocalyptic cooking. It is called, aptly
enough, "bokkura" (muddy mud), and it differs from "bokku," or
regular mud, both in the spelling and in the fact that no one has
eaten it and lived. "Bokkura" is made by placing one "bokku" (literally, "awful muddy thing") on top of another, and then throwing the whole mess over your shoulder, hoping no one notices.

And so we can see that dessert for the troglodytes is very much
like dessert for us, and that one man's meat is another man's poison (literally, "poison").

THE PHILOSOPHER KING CAPER

(From the Casebook of Mike Freeman, America's Only Truly Liberated Detective)

Normally I don't take cases like this. But what's normal about a geek named John Q. Public who has 1.7 kids, 2.2 cars and is between the ages of 18 and 35? When I arrived that morning he was already wearing out what was left of the carpet in the lobby.

My secretary had the day off—in fact, given our recent dispute about the constitutionality of the minimum wage, she had the rest of her life off—so after the introductions I let him into the office myself and sat him down in one of the two beautifully appointed folding chairs. Demographer's dream or not, he was shaking like a paint mixer, except that there were no metallic clamps holding his five-gallon, flat enamel head in place. Suddenly tears and words came pouring out of him in a rush of pent-up emotion.

"I don't know if I can take it anymore, Mr. Freeman," he sobbed.

"Call me Mike," I said, "and you don't have to take it, whatever 'it' is." I reached into the bottom desk drawer and offered him a well-preserved quart of Old Granddad. But neither of us could unscrew the lid from the specimen jar, and the sight of Old Granddad's gaze following us around the room from behind 32 ounces of formaldehyde was pretty creepy, so I put the jar back.

"I think I'm going nuts," he said. "Either that or there's a secret government conspiracy to drive me nuts. But that sounds crazy, doesn't it?"

"Not in my book." I handed him a copy of my book and helped him find the index entry for "Nuts, government trying to drive you."

"I seem to have split into two disparate personalities," he continued.

"No crime there, unless neither of your personalities can afford $200 a day, plus expenses." He grinned.

"Nothing like that. You see, according to every newspaper editorial writer in the country, when I go into a polling place, I'm a philosopher king."

"So?" I lit up a menthol Philosopher King and blew a smoke ring at the miniature plastic hula girl holding down the loose papers on my desk.

"So in an election year, they always say I combine the practical wisdom of Aristotle with the democratic idealism of Thomas Jefferson. Plus they assume I've read more history than Arnold Toynbee, I question everything, I'm familiar with all the issues, I've written my own position papers, I can recite the party platforms backwards, and I've taken the time to get to know each of the candidates personally. Naturally, I assume the same about them."

"Naturally. Aside from your almost crippling sense of self-effacement, however, what's the problem?"

"It's what happens when I leave the voting booth and walk into the supermarket, Mike. According to these same editorial writers, as soon as I stop voting for politicians and start voting with my wallet, I instantly lose 100 IQ points. My mind goes blank. My will withers away. I shuffle like an extra from *Night of the Living Dead,* helplessly controlled by whatever blatantly commercial propaganda flashes in front me. A cartoon dromedary can cause me to inhale poisoned narcotic air. An action movie merchandising tie-in can convince me that a shooting spree is the best way to resolve all conflicts. The richest man in the world can get me to give him more of my money in exchange for a software package that barely works. In short, I become a drooling idiot with no moral center."

"That is a problem, unless you are by profession a newspaper editorial writer," I said. He shook his head sadly.

"I'm just a humble marriage broker. Although I've just bought a controlling interest in Larry King," he added with a touch of pride.

"Let's leave the sordid details of your job out of this and concentrate on the relevant facts, Mr. Public. As a citizen and voter, it appears you are proud, brilliant and independent—what was your phrase?— a philosopher king straight out of Plato's Cave."

"That's right... if you believe all the newspaper editorial writers."

"Like gospel. Yet these same infallible moral lighthouses say that as a consumer, you are a blind cave salamander, a quivering worm, a helpless, ignorant moron incapable of choosing a breakfast cereal without the aid of a corrupt, inefficient, multi-billion-dollar bureaucracy."

"That's it in a nutshell, Mike. Can you solve this one?"

"It's not a one, it's a two," I said.

"Huh?"

"A dichotomy. There's no mystery here. You suffer from Bipolar Buying-Voting Dementia, like every good American. When you vote, you're a genius and whatever you decide is always the best of all possible worlds. When you buy, you're a low-grade numbskull who must be protected from himself at all costs. Oddly enough, that makes you two completely separate individuals who live in the same body yet have nothing to do with each other—unless you happen to be buying votes. Then you are still a genius, but an evil genius."

"Sounds awful. What can I do?"

"Simple. Take this handy portable voting booth that I keep around the office for emergencies just like yours. Strap it to your back, carry it with you at all times, and you'll always be a voter imbued with the wisdom of the ages, not a consumer imbued with the imbecility of the marketplace. And you'll never feel like a bumbling, incompetent yahoo again...until you get married."

"That's very generous of you, Mike, but are you sure you won't be needing this yourself?" I chuckled softly.

"You forget this is Chicago, Mr. Public. You have to be dead 20 years before they'll let you vote. By my count I've still got 14 years to go. Anyway, I gave up voting when I realized it was worse for my health than smoking Cuban cigars, drinking Everclear and playing Russian roulette."

"You mean I've got to wear this thing for two whole decades?" he yelped. "But when do I get to pull the lever?"

"If that's all that's troubling you, I suggest you take the next flight to Las Vegas. They'll let you pull all the levers you want. It's almost exactly like voting, except the odds are better, they take less of your money and at least you get a few laughs along the way."

He looked as happy as Nick Nolte's dealer.

"Gosh, Mike, how can I ever repay you?"

"I prefer bright shiny new Krugerrands, but I'll settle for some old-fashioned silver dollars," I replied.

DID SOMEONE CALL ME SNORER?

Sleep... sweet, sweet, sleep... let it come... the soft fog lowering among the white pines... black waves hissing against the sand... in, and out... in, and out... the unblinking moon in the mist... a sea bird trills gently, distantly... the bird cries... how sad, it says... how beautiful... its voice goes an octave lower... two octaves higher... it gurgles... hiccups... what's *wrong* with that bird?... it makes a sound like a ratchet... getting closer, louder... rasping like a ruptured air hose... now shrieking and swooping... gibbering and—and *laughing!*... flapping horribly—that thing was never meant to fly... oh God, it's not a bird, not a bird but a bug... a great, hideous, jabbering insect... all swirling tendrils and swollen abdomen... a thousand eyes, a thousand mouths—all staring, screaming... blotting out everything...

I bolted upright, gasping. My wife lay next to me. Her snores filled the room with a wash of sound, an alien symphony of whistles, grunts and nasal blasts. When I nudged her she mumbled and turned over, muffling the free concert. I lay back thinking, Where did she get such talent?

From her Uncle George, the one who could smoke cigarettes through his ears? Or the grandfather she wouldn't talk about— what was his name?...

"Grandpa Vlad."

"Jah?" He raised his lidless eyes and looked through me. Hard to believe a gaze that tranquil could hide a broken mind.

"Your soup, Grandpa. Finish your soup." I pushed the bowl toward him and he looked through it. I placed the spoon in his hand and he smiled. He began warbling a little song, accompanying himself by tapping the spoon on his water glass.

"In heaven dere iss no beer, dat's why ve drink it here..." He coughed into his soup.

"Grandpa!"

"Jah, jah sure," he said. He peered into the bowl. "Hello in dere. Anybody home?" When no one answered he dipped his spoon, took a long sip followed by a long breath and, liking the rhythm of it, finished his soup that way—sipping and breathing. The obscene slurping noises he made complemented his cadaverous wheezings, and I found myself listening for which would stop first. But they didn't stop.

He reached the bottom of the bowl and kept going, licking the bowl when his spoon failed to bring up any more. His tongue was incredibly long. I wondered why I had never noticed it before.

"That's enough, Grandpa." The slurping got louder. There was no more soup but he kept sucking frantically, pursing his thick lips into a pulsating "O" like some monstrous pink lamprey. How could he keep inhaling without exhaling? I shivered suddenly and backed away. The slurping was deafening—he held the bowl to his face by sheer force of suction—and then the bowl vanished inside him. His unblinking eyes bulged swiveling from his head as the wind from within him tugged at everything loose in the restaurant: knives, forks, napkins, saltshakers, tablecloths— all flew into the widening hole that had been his face. A busboy screamed, waved his arms and tried to run, but Grandpa got him, sucking him in like a piece of lint.

Then he turned on me. His gaping orifice emitted sounds that should never be heard on this earth. Just as he was reaching for me with his shuddering snout he inhaled one of his own arms. There was a terrible screeching of torn fabric and flesh, and in a moment he sucked himself out of existence, disappearing with an audible pop.

I sat up yelling his name before I knew where I was. I didn't want to be alone then. Shaking my wife to rouse her enough to share my misery, I noticed she wasn't breathing right. She was sleeping on her stomach— something I had never seen her do— and her face was buried in the pillow, twisting back and forth. I turned her over but the pillow came with her, and I had to pull it out of her mouth.

"What are you doing?" she snapped. "Leave me alone!"

"You tried to swallow the pillow."

"So?"

"You were making a noise like a vacuum cleaner in molasses."

"So?"

"So you woke me up."

"*I* woke *you* up? I was only trying to cover my ears. I haven't gotten three minutes of sleep all night with your snoring. You sound like a French horn being played by a rabid howler monkey."

I hit her with the pillow and got up to look at the moon.

A Bare Bodkin, or: One Lunch, Naked, to Go

Once in a millennium, it is an editor's sacred privilege to play midwife to a writer of earthshaking significance and eye-rolling originality. Unfortunately, that hasn't happened to us yet, but until it does we are honored to introduce our readers to Richard Bodkin, or "The San Francisco Earthquake," as he is known to intimates. Mr. Bodkin, our readers; readers, Mr. Bodkin.

For years, Mr. Bodkin has been jotting down odd thoughts at odd moments, using dinner napkins and playing cards for stationery, and then stuffing the scraps into his hatband and losing the hat. Such retiring habits are no boon in the rough-and-tumble arena of literary backslapping and backbiting. Bodkin has never sought after eminence; nor, up to now, has it shown any interest in him.

We hope to change all that. Below are printed, for the first time anywhere, the collected works of Richard Bodkin. Spanning the years 1944 to 1990 ("the prolific period"), they readily demonstrate why Robinson Jeffers referred to Bodkin as "that fat, slobbering stinkbug," and why T.S. Eliot, upon meeting Bodkin for the first time, felt it was an act of simple Christian charity to smother him with a pillow. Luckily for Bodkin, Edna St. Vincent Millay was in the room at the time. After an impassioned argument, she convinced Eliot to give her the pillow, and was attempting to smother Bodkin herself when the police raided the joint.

The Scum Also Rises (an excerpt)

Brad sat in the only café in the little Spanish town and drank a bottle of the local wine. He did this by pouring the wine into a soiled piece of gauze and wringing out the bandage over his face, catching the drops with his tongue as they fell. The gauze had been with him in the War. It was all he had left. That and some chewing tobacco.

"This is a good café," he said in English to the waiter, "and good wine, and I am a very good boy." The waiter smiled that childlike Spanish smile and emptied a pot of coffee into Brad's lap. Brad laughed bitterly at the man's quiet courage. He had been brave once. Now he was a coward. Worse than a coward. A fool. Worse than a fool. In love.

Lady Bitcherly walked in and took the waiter in her arms and kissed him and gave him her room number, saying it loudly and slowly in Spanish. The waiter began to smile that smile again but was interrupted by Brad's wine bottle breaking over his head.

"Good bottle, that," said Lady Bitcherly.

"Good waiter," said Brad. "Why the hell don't we take him up to your room and give him what for?"

"Why the hell not?" she said. He knocked her out and began to drag them both upstairs. This is what war is like, he thought.

Bodkin's first and only novel, of course, went unpublished during his lifetime, like all of his work. Still, he had the admiration of the critics. Edmund Wilson called this manuscript "the sort of thing a carnival pinhead might produce after drinking a gallon of rotgut and spending a weekend on a Tilt-a-Whirl." It was praise like this that kept Bodkin writing until he was struck down several years ago by a trolley car going uphill. He wasn't killed immediately, although the conductor went back over him several times to make sure. He was taken to a trauma center by a squad car, and pronounced dead on arrival by the doctor.

"No, I'm not," he said weakly.

"We'll soon take care of that," replied the doctor, at heart a kind man who couldn't stand the sight of suffering. He administered a dose of strychnine to Bodkin and waited for the results. Bodkin asked for a sheet of paper and a pencil, and in a few moments had composed his only known book of poetry, *To Hell in a Handbasket*.

A Poem

> I think that I shall never see
> A thing as lovely as me.

This somewhat stilted poem was Bodkin's first attempt at verse, and as such is understandably traditional in its rhyme scheme. In his later poems (about three minutes later) Bodkin abandoned rhyme for a verse structure so free as to be promiscuous. As Robert Frost once said of Bodkin's prose works, "If Bodkin's blood could but be spilled / And his mewling forever stilled!" This heartfelt comment applies equally to Bodkin's verse output.

Another Poem

Ha ha! Fooled you, didn't I?

Bodkin rarely showed his sense of humor, and the above poem reveals why. In it, Bodkin anticipated the Beatnik writers, but in typical fashion he was 35 years too late. Because of this, literary historians seldom class him with the Beats, and he is most often classed with the nematodes (in the words of Daniel Webster, "any of a class or phylum of elongated cylindrical worms parasitic in animals or plants or free-living in soil or water").

Yet Another Poem

This time I'm going to write one if it kills m—

Of this last of Bodkin's works, what can be said? *Sic transit gloria mundi.*

The OCD Repeater: A Journal of Understanding

The Obsessive-Compulsive Disorder Repeater ("Bet you can't read it just once!") is published monthly, or sometimes more often if we can't stop ourselves, for victims of OCD. As always, we welcome your letters. Of course, we pledge to reveal only your problem, not your identity. All symptoms discussed here will be considered completely confidential, unless some strange overwhelming urge compels us to scream your name to the world at 10-second intervals.

Dear OCD Repeater:

I am normal in every respect, except for a slight tendency to touch the doorknob with my forehead 500 times each morning before leaving for work. Don't advise me to change my habits. I've already tried making drastic variations in my routine. One morning, for example, I touched my forehead to the doorknob 512 times, but instead of producing the inner peace I have come to depend on, this pointless overindulgence left me feeling jaded and world-weary, as if I were only going through the motions.

The next morning, in a mad mood of defiance, I touched my head to the doorknob only 497 times. At first this gave me a false sense of bravado. As the day progressed, however, the premonition grew on me that I would soon pay for my recklessness—and I did.

When I made my daily stop at the Pig & Swig for a cup of cappuccino at precisely 6:15 a.m., I was told they were out of low-cal nondairy creamer. How they snickered when they saw the panic bubbling behind my eyes! I strived to calm myself by rubbing the secret patch of flannel I carry in my pocket for just such emergencies. I even tried stepping over every third crack in the sidewalk on the way to work, but it was no use. My morning, and quite likely my life, was ruined.

I am getting a bit off the point, though. What I want to say is, Why can't people just leave me alone? I harm no one. I do my job. I pay taxes. Aside from forming a hollow in my forehead so pronounced that my skull is occasionally mistaken for a ceramic planter, my "little hobby" (as I call it) has brought me the only real happiness I've ever known. What's wrong with that?

Soft in the Noggin in New York City

Dear Soft:

Clearly your need to touch your forehead to the doorknob accomplishes nothing of practical value, except perhaps polishing the brass. To be sure, there are many actions we must constantly repeat that do not in themselves constitute obsessive-compulsive disorder. For instance, I find it impossible to get through the day unless I fill my briefs with a mixture of oat bran and cough syrup while humming "Lara's Theme" from Doctor Zhivago. *Surely my reasons are obvious. But does anyone have the slightest idea why you carry on like such a jackass? I don't.*

❋ ❋ ❋ ❋ ❋

Dear OCD Repeater:

Who discovered obsessive-compulsive disorder? And is there a cure? I have a friend who needs to know.

Just wondering in Wheeling, West Virginia

Dear Wondering:

OCD was first diagnosed in 1963 by Dr. Neil Bogusian, who realized that his wife's insatiable need to serve "snapping turtle surprise" and lima beans every night of the year was more a cry for help than a cold-blooded attempt to drive him insane. After having her euthanized by the family vet (Mrs. Bogusian was a dead ringer for a dachshund, and had missed her last two distemper shots anyway), the good doctor devised the original five-step program for alleviating the pain of OCD sufferers:

1. Admit that you have a problem.

2. Admit that you are helplessly in the thrall of some malignant, unseen power that is making you admit you have a problem.

3. Admit that you just added up the number of letters in the above two sentences and subtracted the total from the last four digits of your Social Security number.

4. Sing "There was a boy who had a dog, and Bingo was his name-o" under your breath whenever you see a red object.

5. Repeat steps one through four until the feeling of nameless dread passes.

❋ ❋ ❋ ❋ ❋

Last issue's Case of the Month brought a host of helpful ideas. You'll recall that our correspondent, a Mr. M.L. of Wheaton, Illinois, complained he was unable to cross the street without reciting the Gettysburg Address four score and seven times, and that the strenuous demands of this absolute necessity were consuming more and more of his time, until he started falling asleep on the curb after midnight and being sideswiped by street-sweeping machines.

Some were sympathetic. "I know just how he feels," wrote M.W. of Peoria. "Personally, I can't make it through an intersection without reenacting the Sand Creek Massacre. You wouldn't believe the number of accidents this has caused—or the number of friends I have made." Others were less patient. C.K. of Buffalo wrote, "He ought to thank his lucky stars it's the Gettysburg Address and not a pep talk from the Nuremburg rallies." The best thought came from K.Z. of Des Moines, who suggested a switch from presidential speeches to Scripture passages, preferably John 11:35 ("Jesus wept").

How Am I Driving?

Thank you for calling the Chrome Donkey Truck Co. driver hotline! We really want to know how our drivers are doing, so please share your experience with us by following these directions and answering a few simple questions.

To report a good experience with a Chrome Donkey Truck Co. driver, press 1.

To report a bad experience with a Chrome Donkey Truck Co. driver, press 2.

If your bad experience involved only a verbal altercation or misunderstanding, however disturbing, press 1.

If there was a physical accident of some kind, press 2.

Was it a minor accident? If so, press 1.

If it was a major accident, press 2.

If the accident was so major that you are now in a full body cast and unable to move your hand, ask the attending physician or nurse to press 3 for you.

If the accident was way beyond major and caused third-degree burns over most of your body and face, making speech impossible, try to establish a "one blink for yes, two blinks for no" communication code with your caregivers, and then convey that they should press 4 for you.

If your eyelids are fused together or no longer there, see if you can wiggle your ears (of course we're using "see" in the figurative sense here). If so, try to establish a "one wiggle for yes, two wiggles for no" communication code with your caregivers. Once they have stopped chuckling, convey that they should press 5 for you, and have them do all the button pressing from here on out.

Which of the following came flying through your windshield during the accident? Press the pound key for each item that applies.

- Hubcap.
- Tire iron.
- Tire (fully inflated).
- Tire (exploded).
- Chrome Donkey Truck Co. driver (fully clothed).
- Chrome Donkey Truck Co. driver (partially clothed, partially on fire).
- Chrome Donkey Truck Co. driver (naked and charred).
- Cow (mad).
- Cow (not mad, exactly, but feelings very hurt).
- Other livestock in varying states of emotional distress.
- Barrel of oil.
- Barrel of industrial cyanide (top intact).
- Barrel of industrial cyanide (top breached).
- Crate of dynamite (no blasting caps).
- Crate of dynamite (with blasting caps).
- Large chunks of weapons-grade plutonium.
- Sidewinder missile.

Now press 1 if the driver apologized.

Press 2 if the driver did not apologize, but had a look on his face as if he might be about to.

Press 3 if you can't be sure whether the driver apologized because, as far as you remember, there was no driver.

Press 4 if you can't be sure whether the driver apologized because, as far as you remember, the driver was a wide-eyed orangutan wearing pilot's goggles.

Press 5 if you are a member of the Orangutan Workers Union and are calling to demand safer working conditions for orangutans in general.

Press 6 if you are Chuckles The Orangutan and are looking for your "one banana, two banana" severance package from this morning's horrific 12-vehicle collision.

If you feel the accident was your fault, press 7.

Just kidding! If a Chrome Donkey Truck Co. driver was to blame, press 8.

Next, do you want to take your case to court? If so, press 1.

If you're willing to settle out of court, press 2.

Now press the number with which your desired settlement amount begins.

Finally, press 0 for every zero after the initial digit in your desired settlement amount, or until you see a smile on your attorney's face.

And thank you again for calling the driver hotline at the Chrome Donkey Truck Co., where—when we're not driving over you in a jackknifed, out-of-control 18-wheeler—we're proud to be driving you nuts.

In the Clouds

"I wandered lonely as a cloud," wrote Wordsworth, but as usual he was probably just reaching for the nearest rhyme. There is small reason to suspect that clouds get lonely, for they are hardly ever alone. If anything the average cloud is, like most of us, hurting for a little privacy—a quiet space where he can concentrate on personal growth, perfect his racquetball serve, learn to stop saying "yes" when he means "go to hell," and work on that hard-hitting novel about the nasty but wacky inner world of advertising.

"Where do all these clouds come from?" you ask (not out loud, I hope, or people will shy away from you and you'll be lonelier than any cloud ever was). A scientist will tell you clouds are merely water vapor suspended in the atmosphere. He will tell you that, and then look away in embarrassment, knowing he has told you nothing. He wishes to God he knew something about clouds, but he's too busy tickling white rats with electrodes to find out anything.

The ancient Chinese believed that clouds were the breath of a sleeping dragon. Storm clouds resulted when the dragon had been smoking in bed, while chain lightning, typhoons and tornadoes meant that he had been awakened before he could get a full eight hours. Today, of course, these childish explanations have been discarded, and the modern Chinese are well aware that clouds are the product of wrong-thinking reactionaries conspiring to form a fascist hegemony with the imperialist war-mongering dogs of the West.

Next to Wilhelm Reich's cloud theories, these Chinese ideas look pretty serious. Reich did most of his damage in his chosen field of psychiatry, but in his spare time he did more to cloud the cloud issue than any other man in history. He was convinced that clouds are not always clouds—that sometimes they are accumulations of deadly orgone energy sent by the saucer men to destroy us. What is orgone energy? When asked, Reich would only chuckle cryptically, "You wouldn't want to sprinkle any on your breakfast cereal." According to him it saps our strength and makes us talk and act like Pauly Shore, and sometimes even buy bumper stickers that say "Fishermen Do It After Tying Up Their Loved Ones With High-Test Fish Line."

Reich had an eye for spotting orgone clouds, though glasses later corrected it so he would see only a banana cream pie hovering safely out of reach. When he spied one (a cloud, not a pie) he'd attack it with a device of his own making called a cloud-buster, which looked like a ménage à trois between a heating pipe, a Slinky toy and one of those tinfoil tuxedoes Liberace used to wear. Invariably, when fired upon, the cloud would disperse or drift away, and the final score was always Humanity: 1, Saucer Men: 0.

If only all visionaries were as harmless.

THE BALLAD OF BIGFOOT

(Found in Samuel Taylor Coleridge's Desk by Rudyard Kipling)

The name's Dan O'Brien and I won't be lyin'
    If I say I've seen a thing or two.
I've sailed more than most from coast to coast,
    From the China Sea to Timbuktu.

I've braved many a gale on back of a whale,
    Sent many a fool to Davy's Locker;
Cut sails from the gizzards o' giant lizards
    And still I ain't ready for a rocker.

I've kissed native girls with coral for curls
    And bodies like burnished ivory.
Then after my pleasures I plunder their treasures
    With whiskey and wiles and connivery.

I take their gold to have and to hold
    And leave 'em to sob in their huts.
I've nothin' to do with 'em when I'm through with 'em—
    The Devil take the heathen sluts!

But in all the years passed before the mast
    I never yet knew a creature
As could make me squeal or turn on my heel
    And holler for a preacher,

Unless you're exceptin' that beast of deception
    With a smell like pickled pig's foot,
That hairy mound who howled like a hound
    The fearful name o'—Bigfoot!

My leaking bark was the *Crippled Shark*,
    My crew was two score and ten;
Recruited from middens and debtors' prisons,
    To a man they were desperate men.

We hoisted our ales and lowered the sails
    And pointed her into the sun,
Then to celebrate this affair of state
    Fired the cook from the forward gun.

The sea was clear as a maiden's mirror,
    The sky was blue as a vein;
We were three days south when the weather gave out
    And began the cursed rain.

It hailed cats and dogs and poisonous frogs
    Till we thought we were Noah's Ark.
Then the mainmast split when the lightning spit
    And crippled the *Crippled Shark*.

We were tossed and torn around the Horn,
    All the while the deck was burning,
But I swore allegiance to the regions
    From which there's no returning.

When the hurricane ceased and gave us peace
    We all of us made crosses,

Then dropped a rope near the Cape o' No Hope
    To ascertain our losses:

One bosun burned, or so I learned
    When I breathed in half his ashes;
The first mate hid 'neath a lifeboat lid
    Till I gave him forty lashes.

The cabin boy had been thrown like a toy
    Behind the fo'c's'le ladder,
And there he stayed while the thunder played
    And he lost control of his bladder.

"Press on!" says I. "We'll do or we'll die,
    And woe to them that disobey.
The first to utter a cowardly mutter
    Will be the first to lose his toupée!"

Though my crew of fifty were yellow and shifty
    And wouldn't stand my scrutiny,
I settled their hash with musket and lash
    Till they planned a murderous mutiny.

They brought me a broth of boiled sloth
    To make me sleep like a gypsy;
Then the second mate took a silver plate
    And bashed me until I was tipsy.

They set me adrift in a scurvy skiff
    With my noggin nailed to the floor
And said, "Roses are red, but dead is dead
    And we'll never see you no more."

The tropical air baked me medium rare,
    To the four winds I was a slave;
And while I was waitin' I prayed to Satan
    To take my crew to the grave.

For days without number I had no slumber
    Nor food, nor drink to tide me by,
And should things get dull a passing gull
    Would make a pass at my one good eye.

By luck at last my bones were cast
    Upon a sharp and slimy beach
Where on the sand a moth-eaten band
    Of monkeys gabbled, each to each.

Monstrous they were with matted fur,
    Faces smiling like open sores;
Such was their stench that it gave me a wrench:
    "Touch me not or you're damned!" I roars.

But worst of all, though their heads were small
    And fit like nuts for cracking,
Their feet were the size of Victoria's thighs—
    No use to try attacking.

Odoriferous, Lord! A vociferous horde,
    They stammered and stank all about me,
Then tried to unmind me by pointing behind me
    When one of 'em made to clout me.

'Twas my belief that she was their chief
    (If such could be anointed);

Each toe was big as a suckling pig
    And her tiny skull was pointed.

In midair she stopped, to her knees she dropped
    And kissed my offended fingers.
I've since washed and washed at a near-fatal cost
    Yet still the smell of her lingers.

"By chance," she queried, "would you be married?
    And if you're not, are you looking?
Unless you're my beau, your carcass we'll throw
    Into that pot a-cooking."

She showed me a stew where my traitorous crew
    Were turned into appetizers.
My men, once vicious, were now delicious
    And none of them the wiser.

"In every port," I says in retort,
    "I've got a gal I call my wife
And more's the pity 'cause they're all pretty
    With looks not like to shorten my life.

"In any event your lovely scent
    Leaves something to be desired.
I'd sooner be buried than getting married
    To an animal that's expired!"

At this she rears and covers her ears
    And screams to have me skewered.
Though few the men within her ken
    She seems to want one fewer.

But I offers my knee completely free
    To her dainty knob of a nose;
Then as if by chance I dances a dance
    On all twelve of her swollen toes.

And before the twits could gather their wits
    I parted 'em like the ocean
And rendered 'em gutless with dagger and cutlass
    To prove my undying devotion.

Without looking back I beat a track
    To the brink of the Devil's waters
And diving headfirst I swore a curse
    On Darwin and all his daughters.

It was sink or swim and by God's whim
    I sunk straight down to the bottom
Where my bones were sweet with delicate meat
    For all the sharks that got 'em.

When next I awoke I was coughing up smoke
    And tied to a bed o' fire;
The name's Dan O'Brien and now I'm lyin'
    Where everyone's a liar.

BONEHEADS

September 14—Africa at last! After weeks of preparation and days of nausea aboard rickety twin-engine prop planes and even more rickety jeeps, we reached the famed Olduvai Gorge, where some of the earliest known human remains have been discovered. My excitement at arriving was tempered by the realization that Professor Donaldson is here also, seeking evidence for his asinine theory that the earliest humans possessed the secret of sheer pantyhose. To my colleague Dr. Rollo and myself, on the other hand, it is apparent that the first humanoids perished precisely because of the lack of proper leggings. Professor Donaldson crashed our arrival celebration and argued his point by giving a disgustingly graphic demonstration of what early man might have looked like in nylons. Meanwhile, I had our cook fill his pith helmet with dung beetles. When he put it back on the beetles believed they had found a mother lode of their favorite food and attacked his bald cranium savagely. He ran off screaming, but I fear we haven't seen the last of him.

September 16—A good day. After scrabbling in the dust of Olduvai for nearly 11 hours and finding nothing besides an Oh Henry! wrapper dating from approximately the mid-1970s, I suddenly came upon part of a humanoid tibia. I haven't properly dated it yet, but my initial guess is that it is at least four million years old. If not, then it may be part of the remains of our driver, who was pecked to death by hummingbirds two days ago—a brutal ordeal lasting almost 24 hours (the African hummingbird is somewhat larger and meaner than its North American cousin). Either way, it is a significant find. I celebrated by sharing a bottle of champagne with our crew. They were rather subdued until Dr. Rollo stepped on a scorpion and started doing a fair imitation of the local fire dance. This put the men in jolly spirits for the remainder of the night, and we all went to bed with smiles on our faces.

September 17—Professor Donaldson snuck past the native guards and into our camp once again, spoiling an otherwise pleasant breakfast of ostrich eggs and python strips. Somehow word of yesterday's find had already leaked out, and of course he had to come sniffing around, the meddling fool. I showed it to him nonetheless and asked his professional opinion out of courtesy more than anything else. He snorted and said that, far from being four million years old and humanoid, it appeared to him to be four weeks old and canine. He then offered to trade me his recent "find" for it: a soft, pliable bone with bits of flesh still attached, which he claimed was from a perfectly preserved pterodactyl, though he could not explain how he came to be carrying it in a Kentucky Fried Chicken box. I declined his offer and had our headman Yobi show him the fast route to the bottom of the gorge—the one with the missing rung on the rope ladder. Hopefully he won't trouble us again.

September 18—Today I began serious work on the ancient tibia fragment. My first attempt at carbon dating was disappointing, giving a result of less than 100 years. But assuming a modest margin of error of only 99.99 percent, this could be interpreted as supporting my hypothesis. I would guess this specimen to be a female—call her "Louise"—because of her coyness about her exact age. In size and general appearance she no doubt resembled Danny DeVito, although she didn't shave as often and almost certainly never starred in any major Hollywood productions. Her diet probably consisted of whatever insects flew into her open mouth. Fake fur was not an option, so she wrapped herself in real animal skins. Her embarrassment at this faux pas would explain why she spent her days hiding in caves—either that or the lack of a reliable sun block and skin moisturizer.

September 20—Another amazing discovery! At the bottom of Olduvai this morning I uncovered a nearly complete male skeleton from the same species as Louise. Because I found it near Professor Donaldson's discarded hat and shoes, I think it only fair that, despite our professional differences, I name it after him: Homo habilis donis. Like Louise, this proto-man had a cranial capacity roughly half the modern average. I'm sure if he were alive today he'd be either a teamster or a human resources manager. What's more, I feel certain that "Donnie" (as I already affectionately refer to him) lacked the power of speech. Most likely in a conversation he was the one nodding his head and going, "Mmm-hmm." He probably communicated by a complex series of grunts, gestures and whistles, not unlike English soccer fans.

September 23—The local police have arrested me, either for the murder of Professor Donaldson or for littering, depending on how their analysis of the recently discovered humanoid skeleton turns out. The fools! They can imprison my body but not my mind. While awaiting trial in their hastily assembled kangaroo court (the kangaroos are being flown in overnight from Australia via FedEx), I began excavating my cell. My cellmates soon joined in, but lacking a spirit of scientific inquiry they preferred to tunnel sideways rather than down, using my head as a combination battering ram-shovel. Within a few hours they made good their escape, leaving me no worse for wear except that my neck has disappeared and I cannot stop saying, "Welcome to McDonald's, may I take your order please?" Yes, the end is near. I can feel my life force ebbing away from me. Or possibly it is just saliva leaking out of a mouth that no longer closes properly. My final act, once I make this last diary entry with my remaining good arm, will be to arrange my limbs so that they will create a positive first impression when some paleontologist from the future digs me up. If there's anything I hate it's a messy excavation site.

TSK OF THE D'URBERVILLES

In the bright, grassy Midlands of England rises the slightly fictional county of Wesson—a dark ink spot of tragedy among the happily blank pages that surround it. The air is heavier there, oppressive with the sense of eternal sadness and inescapable gloom. The sun does not shine on Wesson, for it has been banned by municipal decree. Neither flowers nor any other living things will bloom there, and the plowmen who homeward plod their weary way raise only Druidic stones from their cursed ash-gray fields. These stones their bony wives bake into a rough black bread very good for the soul but very bad for the teeth. Even this hard fare is thought too kingly by some of the sterner natives, who would rather suck an ice cube than eat a pagan meal. The inhabitants of Wesson know it is no use. They have given up.

Birds will not fly over the county, and the Wesson birds themselves don't fly at all, remaining stoically perched in the bare trees that blight the countryside. Only when pierced by a sudden, ineluctable sorrow will they cry out, and then only with a mournful death-shriek as they plummet heartbroken to the ground. It was just such a luckless fowl that fell upon the brow of Tsk Durbeyfield where she sat weeping beneath a petrified oak. Though partly concussed and no child of fortune herself, Tsk took the rook in her arms and crooned a pitiful prayer into its dead eyes.

But the bird was not yet dead. With amazing alacrity it rallied to her tune and in its dying frenzy fastened its beak on her nose.

For the world is as cruel as its maker, and He cares not a fig if a crow should peck a girl's face off—even so beautiful a face as Tsk's.

Without quite knowing why, she was ashamed. She had not sinned, but she was guilty. After all, there was a dead bird hanging from her nose, and that sort of thing simply was not done in Wesson—at least not in polite society. Like a woodland creature, Tsk knew instinctively that she was the living antithesis of Victorian hypocrisy and repression, yet she also sensed dimly, like the House of Lords, that through a succession of historically inevitable degradations her bucolic existence was fated to end in unearned suffering. And it occurred to her what a smashing novel it all would make, if only Jackie Collins had published in the 19th century, or Thomas Hardy in the 21st.

Then she thought of her family—of her father, Mr. Durbeyfield, known somewhat enigmatically as "Sir Speedy"; of her mother, known even more enigmatically as "Mrs. Durbeyfield"; and of her four younger sisters, Liza Lu, Little Lulu, Lockjaw and Old Black Joe. How could she face them now? She laughed bitterly when she recalled their despicable poverty. Why, they were so poor they could not even afford to give her a middle name, and she had to use her first name twice: Tsk Tsk. Was it any wonder she had fallen so far from grace? With girlish simplicity she reflected on the combination of socioeconomic factors that had run her like a rabbit into the briar bush of morality. It was all so confusing! Perhaps Lucifer Jones could help her unravel it. Dear Lucifer—so good, so strong...and so deathly dull. She covered her face with her burlap shawl and went to him.

"Tsk!" he exclaimed. "How good to see you at the vernal equinox. Isn't it grand? I've developed a new method of corn blight control. Shall I tell you about it?" He did, and she fell asleep instantly. As he gazed at her veiled charms he felt a reckless impulse to make a new type of feed sack out of her shawl. But when he pulled the coarse cloth back from her face he recoiled in disgust.

"You—you aren't the woman I loved," he stammered.

"Then who am I?" Tsk replied huskily, like an ear of corn.

"Another woman in her shape, with a feathered carcass attached to her proboscis." Though only a simple millionaire's son, he knew his Latin, and could conjugate dead verbs in a way that melted a girl's heart. Tsk wept anew as Lucifer strode briskly away from her.

"Where are you going?" she cried.

"To invent some new sort of threshing device made out of human teeth—but also to find a girl who doesn't consort with dead specimens of any of various large glossy black oscine birds of the family Covidae and especially the genus Corvus. Farewell!"

Tsk, wounded to her soul, took comfort in the knowledge that she was not merely a backward Durbeyfield but an atavistic d'Urberville, one of a long degenerate line of anemic aristocrats whose skeletons rotted in decrepit Wesson tombs. How soothing this secret was! For when all was said and done the d'Urbervilles were only Durbeyfields, and the Durbeyfields only d'Urbervilles, and in the eyes of God neither mattered more than a dead crow.

Limestone Luxury Condos

There's a new feeling underfoot here in Quagmire, Florida, and the new feeling is... there's *nothing* underfoot!

Thanks to a patented process called Irreversible Desiccation, great hollows have opened underneath our former residents to make room for you, and you, and millions more just like you—sleek young professionals with Tennis Elbow and Smartphone Pinky, tender but tough, youthful but useless. Sinkhole & Sons Realty is looking for glistening Caucasian physiques in fishnet underwear just tight enough to hurt. For tanned bodies like yours that pose almost naturally, almost believably in the latest styles driving the latest cars ("The Predator," "The Quasi-Motors Hunchback") and drinking the latest drinks ("The Vodka Valium").

Quagmire used to be the place where everyone with nowhere else to go had to go, but they're all gone now, all of them. All the pensioners without the strength to endorse their ludicrously insufficient checks. All the unshaven old men and unshaven old women who used to shuffle from trash container to trash container saying, "I remember... I remember..." when of course they couldn't remember *anything,* not even their next of kin. All gone now. One minute they were standing helplessly in their shallow sandy gardens, propping themselves up with hoes and rakes and saying, "I remember... I remember..." The next minute, as if by divine fiat, the earth opened beneath them, and in place of the elder ones stood a new development in modern living from Sinkhole & Sons: Limestone Luxury Condos.

If you've ever wanted to live like a blind cave salamander, groping for sightless white grubs in the slimy primordial dark, Limestone Luxury Condos could be for you. Close to Hell yet within praying distance of Heaven, these subterranean cavern units are also convenient to shopping at the ultra-modern Manglers Mall, where you will be treated like an honored prisoner of war by the brightly outfitted security personnel. Whether you eat your heart out at the Self-Serve Organ Surplus Warehouse, or mix metaphors and partners at the First Circle Bar and Grill ("Dante's Bottomless and Topless Pit Stop"), you'll appreciate the impersonal air of affluence that washes over you at Manglers Mall.

Get beneath it all. Come to Limestone Luxury Condos and sink out of sight with us into a spectral world where all necessities and toiletries must be lowered by rope. Listen to the mineral-laden water bleeding in from above as it drips endlessly from magnificently contorted ceilings onto pitted prehistoric floors, heedless of human concerns, ignorant of the latest fashions in jogging clothes, seeking only the warmth and quietude of the earth's core.

The Lesser Song of Songs, Which Is Sheba's

(After the Manner of King James)

Let him not kiss me with the kisses of his mouth: for thy tongue is as a lizard's tail, which pulled off doth regrow tenfold. Nor yet with the kisses of his nose, for thy nose runneth over. Nor yet with the kisses of his ears: for thou art truly weird to ponder such a thing.

Thine ointments cleave to me, and their savour doth repel insects and anything that breathes; yea, even the Shittites avoid me, and I cannot get a table at the palace cafeteria.

I have compared thee, O my love, to a herd of mountain goats leaping from a cliff: the sound of their skulls when they land is sweet and comely. Behold, thou art fair, my beloved, yea, pleasant, nay, bland as a potato baked in polyunsaturated fats: also thy concubines are tax-deductible.

A bundle of old clothes for Amvets is my beloved unto me; he shall lie all night bewtixt my breasts, not knowing what to do with them.

2

Stay me with flagstones, comfort me with knockout drops: for I am sick of love. His left hand is under my head, but his right hand doth embrace himself.

120

The voice of my beloved! Behold, he cometh leaping on toe shoes, skipping like a gigolo, tripping on his hem. Verily, he hath borrowed my eye makeup once too often.

My beloved is like a white, white rat: behold, he standeth behind our wall looking for table scraps, he looketh forth at the windows when I dress, shewing himself through the lattice.

My beloved is mine, and I am his, yea, though we file separately.

3

By night on my bed I sought him whom my purse loveth: I sought him, but I found him not. I sought him under the bed, but I found him not. I sought him in my closet, and there I thought I found him trying on my silks, but it was only a mannequin.

I will rise now, and go about the city in the streets carrying a shopping bag full of old bus transfers and speaking to myself. I will seek him whom my purse loveth, for he must cosign my checks.

The watchmen that go about the city beating anything that moves found me; to whom I said, Saw ye him whom my purse loveth? They smiled and pointed to their foreheads, nodding sagely like my beloved.

4

Behold, thou art fair, my love: thou hast a set of Mediterranean bedroom eyes, of simulated walnut, marked down 60 percent for the holidays. Thy hair hath been washed in the blood of the lamb, but thou hast forgot to rinse.

Thy tooth shines in the night like a piece of eggplant on the bald dome of the Pharaoh.

The smell of thy garments is like unto the smell of Gary, Indiana with all of the chief spices: oregano, jalapeño and monosodium glutamate.

5

Thy nose is as the tower of Sears which looketh toward Skokie.

6

I try to sleep, but my heart waketh: it is the voice of my beloved that knocketh like a bottle launching a ship, saying, Open to me, my love, for my head is filled with good wine and evil thoughts. But I moved my dresser in front of the door and he went away.

My beloved put in his hand by the hole of the door, but I slapped it. My drawers were not moved for him, and he went away.

The watchmen that went about the city stomping anything that wriggles found me, they smote me, they pushed me into some sweet-smelling goulash; the keepers of the walls took away my veil from me. Then they screamed and gave it back.

SPEECH, SPEECH!

In the 34 years it has been my pleasure to be associated with this company—well, not quite 34, actually, but very close to it, very close indeed—in fact, a good deal more than 33—perhaps even more than 33 and a half, though I'm not sure, it might have been a leap year—but anyway, so close to 34 that it might as well *be* 34, even though it's *not*—at least, I don't think so...As I was saying: In the 33 (or possibly 34) years I've been associated with this company—and may I add that the association has always been a pleasurable one—of course I'm only speaking for myself, but in a sense, as president of this firm I speak for all of us when I say that the pleasure associated with my association with the company—or strictly speaking, the company's association with *me*—has always been a great source of pleasure. Which is not to imply that it is not still a great source of pleasure—not at all—indeed, the continuation of the association will always continue to provide a continued source of pleasure—a very great source—for the company—or me, rather—or at any rate, *someone.* I hope.

As I look out over this crowd of eager faces—I think they're faces—I mean, I think they're eager—I say, as I eagerly face these equally eager faces—a crowd of them, mind you, and I remember the days when there were only a handful of us here, only a few—three, it was, unless you count Mrs. Kaiser, my personal secretary—that would make it four—I guess we really *ought* to count her, since she did all the work—stand up, Mrs. Kaiser, stand up, dear—I'm sorry, she can't stand up, apparently, she broke her hip or something—of course if she had told me sooner I would've given her some time off, although technically she doesn't have any coming to her until later this year—*next* year, I should say— that is, the next *fiscal* year...The point is, we had to wear a lot of hats back then, way back when it all started 34—33, really— years ago. No, it *must* have been 34, because that was the year Uncle Leopold fell down the stairs—I mean, the *first* time he fell down the stairs—I think he was only doing it for fun after that, trying to keep busy, you know—worked until he was 98. Of course he had to, we were charging him rent, and that man knew how to eat—I mean, you'd put one slice of bread on his plate and in no time at all he'd be asking for another—a hell of a man, Uncle Leopold was, a hell of a man—talk about a sense of humor, why he could make you laugh at nothing. Right out of the blue he'd say: "I'm going to smoke until it kills me. I've got nothing to live for." Then he'd light up and we'd all burst out laughing.

He had another trick, too—did I ever tell you this story?—I guess not. We'd hide his checks—you know, pension, social secu- rity, whatever came for him—and then we'd make him look for them. He'd play along just like a true sport and pretend to search everywhere, days at a time—and then he'd give up. I can still see him standing at the top of the stairs, bawling his eyes out as if he really cared about those checks—of course he *didn't*—he didn't need them, he had $300 saved in one of his socks—we took it one month when he couldn't make the rent, but we put play money in there so he wouldn't know the difference—uh—

Where was I again?

The IMF Good-as-Gold Card

Dear Third World Dictator or Corrupt, Impotent Figurehead of a Failed Pseudo-Democracy:

Not everyone deserves the IMF Good-as-Gold Card. It's designed especially for nations that know how to make other people responsible for their debts. Nations that know spending other people's money is always spending wisely. Nations with a timely, regular record of complete nonpayment. It's these special nations, like your own, that deserve to be pre-approved and pay less for the card that never stops giving.

Our rate is the lowest in the known universe: a negative 6.9% APR. That's right—simply by acquiring our card you will start earning money, because any outstanding loans will decrease at the rate of 6.9% a year until Bono manages to convince everyone they should be wiped off the books. And you can be certain that this rate will never change, regardless of changes in the Prime Rate, the global market, or the structure of reality itself.

Your credit line is limited only by Heisenberg's Uncertainty Principle and by your ability to add a string of zeros to the right of a "1" (if you haven't yet mastered this essential skill of international finance, our trained advisors will be only too glad to show you how).

A credit line of this magnitude allows you to buy what you want when you want it. What is your country's main need? Transportation (new Mercedes for mistress)? Education (singing coach for mistress)? Infrastructure (facelift for mistress)? Health (penicillin shots for mistress)? Whatever it may be, you'll find that the IMF Good-as-Gold Card opens a whole world of spending possibilities for you.

With an APR this low, you can save by transferring your countless smaller bad loans into one gigantic consolidated bad loan. Why go through the monthly hassle of defaulting on all those nickel-and-dime debts when you can default on one easy, unimaginably large debt?

Unlike many other gold cards, which charge an annual fee of up to $75, the IMF Good-as-Gold Card has no annual fee. In fact, we'll pay you $75 million right now just to take it.

Even better are the IMF Good-as-Gold Card's many other benefits. For instance, our Emergency Next-Day Credit Line Two-For-One Policy, which automatically doubles your credit limit if your card is lost or stolen. And you can call our 24-hour Customer Service Center for help at any time to hear a prerecorded message from Bono about the importance of spending money like a drunken sailor. If it's an emergency, you can also speak directly to an actual IMF Good-as-Gold Card representative about the vital need to spend money like there's no tomorrow.

So be sure to take advantage of this extraordinary pre-approved and eternally non-rescindable offer today. An insanely low negative 6.9% APR. A credit line higher than Madonna's hem. Guaranteed savings that will continue until the heat death of the universe. And the kind of service only a highly motivated, lifelong bureaucratic corps can offer. What does it all add up to? A card only certain nations deserve: The IMF Good-as-Gold Card.

Sincerely,

Daniel P. Frothenmouth
Marketing Manager
International Monetary Fund

P.S. You deserve more, so call now for your pre-approved IMF Good-as-Gold Card with no annual fee (except to the American taxpayer) and a negative 6.9% APR. Please take a moment right now to fill out and return the attached Bank-So-Big-It-Must-Not-Fail Acceptance Agreement, along with the Debt-So-Large-It-Can-Never-Be-Repaid Waiver of Responsibility. Or you could just wait a while. After all, if Bono has his way, this special offer will never expire.

Los Perros Bravos! Or, Death at Teatime

(With No Apologies Whatsoever to Ernest Hemingway)

At the first dogfight I ever attended I expected to be horrified and sickened by what I had heard would happen to the horses. I had been told that what happened to the horses would make me cry and spit up like a *niño* (little child), even though I am not a *niño*. What happened to the horses, I had been warned, would make my *nalgas* (buttocks) quiver like those of a *maricon* (fairy), even though I am not a *maricon*. I am an *hombre* (man). *Un hombre mucho macho* (very masculine) *con muchos cojones* (many testicles). I lost one or two *cojones* in the War, but that is another story which is neither here nor there and I will not tell it to you. I will only mention the War in such a way that you will know I was in it, and then I will tell you what I know of the dogfights in Madrid in the spring when the air is clean and cool and an *hombre* may drink four bottles of wine and only pay for three, for there is no place on earth like Madrid in the spring and the only dogfights worth seeing happen in Madrid and the only time they are worth seeing is in the spring. *Comprende?*

I had heard about the horses (*los caballos* we call them in Spain), about the tragedy of their suffering in the *plaza de perros* (the dog ring to you *turistas*). I was delighted to discover that nothing more happens to the horses than happened to me during the War. They are merely disemboweled, and the disemboweling is done so cleanly and so coolly and with such an air of good humor that one cannot help but smile as one smiled at the Kaiser. It is the exact opposite of tragedy to see the horses trot into the ring with the *picadors* on their backs dressed in bright red polka-dot costumes and wearing red rubber noses and carrying pickaxes, and then to see the *picadors* swing their picks into one another's horses and the suddenly red horses falling on their riders and the *picadors* all killed or maimed in a way that makes everyone smile, some of them crushed instantly, others left to die in the sand from their concussions, for that is the sort of thing that happens to one if one happens to be a *picador* or a horse in Madrid in the spring. Madrid, by the way, is the best place to see the dogfights, unless you wish to go the extra distance to Valencia, where the air is cleaner and so cool that you will have to wear your mittens and the water is so clear that you can see through it and even the natives will bathe in it if you hold a gun to their heads and smile. The dogfights in Valencia make the dogfights in Madrid look like a slumber party for interior decorators.

After the *picadors* and the horses have been carried off by an honor guard of *bastardos* (favorite sons), the dogfight begins in earnest. The Spanish, by the way, have no word equivalent to our dogfight, and refer to the event as *la corrida de perros* (literally, a running of dogs, or in Cuba, running dog lackeys of the imperialist stooges).

The band plays a march, and very badly, too, and the three *doggieadors* (dog killers) enter the ring wearing red rubber pants and the little tri-cornered hats folded from yesterday's newspapers. If the music is happy they skip gaily around the arena while the crowd shouts its approval and throws *botellas* (bottles); otherwise, if the music is sad, they hold hands solemnly and approach the presidential box, where *el presidente* jabs each one in the eye with his forefinger and calls them *hijos de putas,* a term of such respect that I will not translate it for you. Temporarily blinded, the *doggieadors* stagger to the center of the ring, each crying *"Mi ojo! Mi ojo!"* (my eye, my eye!). The blinding is mainly symbolic of the Inquisition and, to a lesser extent, of God's pact with Abraham, but it is also meant to even the chances between man and dog at the Moment of Truth.

The dog, meanwhile, has been kept in complete isolation prior to the fight. His teeth have been cleaned, his coat trimmed, and his *cojones* tied off with twine to give him more of an edge. Only a cowardly *doggieador,* a real schoolgirl, will fight an immature or sickly or ill-bred dog. The ideal fighting animal is a pure-blooded adult Chihuahua standing a full seven or eight inches at the shoulders and showing nails at least half an inch long. It is true that in certain towns, like Valencia, the authorities have given in to the public outcry from fairies and ballerinas and dog-fighting is no longer the manly art it once was. In such places they fight Chihuahuas whose nails have been clipped to almost nothing and the *doggieadors* wear hard hats instead of the traditional paper hats, thus entirely avoiding the Moment of Truth. But that is only in Valencia, where the toughest *hombre* in town could not beat up your grandmother and you would have to beat her up yourself. For a real dogfight, the kind your grandmother knew, you must go all the way to Seville, where the air is so clean you can bathe in it and so cool that you can walk around all day with a block of ice on your head and the ice will not melt and the *putas* will charge you less because they can count only as many pesos as they have fingers. The dogfights in Seville make the dogfights in Valencia look like a petting zoo full of tranquilized hamsters.

When the *doggieadors* have partially recovered their eyesight and are moaning quietly to themselves, a *muchacho* (little bastard) lights the firecracker that has been tied to the dog's tail. The explosion scares everyone, especially the dog, who will run in circles trying to bite what's left of his tail. Before he knows what has happened the dog's antics have brought him to the *doggieadors,* who by this time have got to their feet and are trying to skip gaily around the arena once more, but the heartiness has gone out of it and they know it.

The dog advances with a death-growl rumbling deep in its throat. The *doggieadors* freeze in their tracks and suddenly the crowd is very, very still. No one breathes. The Moment of Truth is at hand. With a fierce, primitive cunning, the Chihuahua licks the feet of one of the dog killers, and says "Yip!" In two shakes of a tall tale, the three *doggieadors* have skewered the dog on their fencing foils and are roasting him over the fire that has just broken out in the stands. *"Chinga tu madre!"* yells the crowd (roughly, honor thy mother). The *doggieadors* respond good-naturedly with *"Besa mi huevos!"* (kiss my eggs, or in this context, our eggs, the eggs of all good citizens).

And so it is over at last and you feel very fine and the bottles are empty and your pockets have been picked and the dog is dead. Is it right? Is it wrong? Who knows? I know only that what is moral is what you feel good after and what is immoral is what you feel bad after and judged by these moral standards the dogfight is very moral to me because I feel very fine while it is going on and have a feeling of life and death and mortality and immortality and solvency and insolvency, and after it is over I feel very sad but also very fine and dandy. That's when I can put the gun to my head and smile and say to the world, *"Besa mi huevos!"*

The Vulgar Boatman, or: One Potato, Two Potato

The following play marks the first appearance in English by the brilliant young dramatist Basil Dung. Mr. Dung *is* English, but by a court order *(People of the United States vs. Dung)* all of his works to date have been translated into ancient Egyptian to keep them out of the hands of children. Since the ban was lifted, Mr. Dung has graciously consented to translate his most famous play into English again. After seeing it, the editors are taking up a collection to have it translated back into ancient Egyptian, where they hope it will remain.

DRAMATIS PERSONAE:

ALFREDO The human gyroscope

TARTINI A man trapped in another man's body

SACCO AND VANZETTI Two innocent bystanders

THE EMERSON QUARTET The Emerson Quartet

MAXWELL An usher

MICHAEL An archangel

WARING A blender

OTHELLO A bellhop

ACT ONE

The time is 8 p.m. on a murky stage in New York. Two starving actors are silhouetted in the moonlight streaming through an unrepaired roof. They are lying stage right, moaning and holding their stomachs. Every few minutes they stop to cut out pictures of food from a women's magazine. As if by accident the first one speaks.

TARTINI: Anyone here have change for a twenty? Just asking, of course.

In the meantime, Alfredo has died and been given a full military funeral. The curtain falls on Tartini, killing him instantly. A voice announces that there will be refreshments served in the lobby, and then we hear a blood-curdling laugh. End of Act One.

ACT TWO

The same stage a few minutes later. Most of the audience has been poisoned, but not so you'd notice. A light spring rain wafts through the hole in the roof. As if through a cheesecloth, an old song-and-dance man barks these words:

OLD SONG-AND-DANCE MAN: Program! Get your red-hot program here! Can't tell the action without a program!

No one answers. He exits stage left, a disillusioned and embittered man. Enter the Emerson Quartet, playing crab soccer and Haydn's *Opus Number Two in E Major.* They are drunk. After falling into the orchestra pit, they lie down and go to sleep. Eventually, some attendants dump them into shopping carts and roll them backstage, where we hear a sudden burst of gunfire. All this time Sacco and Vanzetti have been in the second balcony stuffing detonator caps into potatoes. Sacco leans over to Vanzetti to whisper something in his ear and Vanzetti breaks out laughing. Then he whispers to Sacco and Sacco does the same. Apparently it is some private joke between the two of them.

ACT THREE

A flourish of trumpets. Enter two heralds.

FIRST HERALD: The King!

SECOND HERALD: *(as if hit from behind with a pipe wrench)* King? *What* King?!?

The curtain is lowered for several months while repairs are begun on the roof, but it is no use, the Revolution can never succeed now.

ACT FOUR

An usher named Maxwell limps onstage to announce that the play is about to begin, and suddenly there is a rush for the lobby. Time passes. The continents continue to drift. Soon the Christmas holidays are at hand. Maxwell crawls back onstage and says that curtain time will be any minute now. There is a note of urgency, perhaps even of warning, in his voice. Somehow we know he will not live to see Paris. The gods become angry. We hear the rumble of distant thunderclouds—or perhaps not so distant. Through the still-open hole in the roof, lightning suddenly strikes a man in the first row, but amazingly, his watch still works. From the wings, a clothing dummy delivers Hamlet's soliloquy in Pig Latin, while an aging custodian pushes a dry mop across the stage. There is not a dry eye left in the house.

Songs of the Renaissance

The recently revealed Da Vinci notebooks have yielded a wealth of information about life in Renaissance Italy. The Da Vinci in question, of course, is not Leonardo but Ricco, the "Amorous Plumber of Rome," who discovered the cold shower and other milestones in personal hygiene. While most of Ricco's notebooks contain nothing more than girl's addresses and sketches saying "Kilroy Was Here," there are some surprises. He was an avid collector of folk songs and ballads, and filled many pages with lyrics from the popular tunes of his day. Usually they were brief (but not brief enough) and told some sort of story (stop me if you've already heard it). Even now, they sound like hits.

The Cheese-Seller's Lament

An old cheese-seller limps down a street in Naples crying, "My cheese is good (gouda), will no one buy it? Unhappy am I, for my boots are full of provolone, and there is no room for my tired feet. My cheese is soft to the touch, like a baby's brow, and many fine molds grow quietly upon it. Oh, who will purchase the cow's treasure?" He continues this way for several hours, until he slips on something and cracks his skull on a lamppost.

Even My Wig Grows Bald When You Are Near

Pepito, a young gallant, enters the courtyard beneath his loved one's window. It is early morning, about two a.m. The young man begins to sing, accompanying himself on a lute badly out of tune. He catches his fingers in the strings and yelps with pain the following words: "Even my wig grows bald when you are near, my love. Oh, my fingers! Oh, my poor fingers!" A girl appears at the window and shouts something indistinguishable. The young man smiles and says: "So great is my love, I tip my wig to you," at which point he pulls out two huge handfuls of his own hair, nearly knocking himself unconscious with the lute. The girl throws down her hand mirror as a symbol of her ardor, but it shatters on the fellow's head. "Oh, my wig!" he says, alternating this with "Oh, my fingers!" The girl is so touched that she drops a small chair squarely onto the boy's back where, like his heart, it breaks. He is almost prostrate with passion. "My name is Pepito, my name is Pepito," he moans. "I think I am dying." "Shut that damn noise!" chimes a voice from across the way, and a shower of beautiful tableware follows. Several forks and knives apparently find their mark, and for once Pepito is speechless. Only the sound of still-resonating lute strings fills the air. After a brief pause, the girl shoves a maplewood dresser over the balcony, and a moment later Pepito is blotted from view. The clock strikes three. Finally, all is quiet.

March of the Maggots

A warm summer evening in Florence. The nightingales sing over the soft a cappella of the crickets as the breeze caresses the olive branches. Soon a horde of maggots crawls into town, drunk and behaving very badly. Their coarse, brutal laughter awakens sev-

137

eral residents. A bottle breaks, and another. Who will pick up the glass? The maggots howl their drunken abuse, as if to say, "Not us!" They recite several off-color limericks and fall down a lot, which is hard for a maggot to do because he is not really standing up to begin with. Then, just as day breaks and the east turns pale crimson and blue, they are crushed beneath the heels of a sad old cheese-seller who is not looking where he is going.

Contest Rules

OFFICIAL RULES: To enter the Bow Wow! Cancun Second Honeymoon Getaway Contest, simply buy a specially-marked can of Econo-Meat Dog Food and scratch off the Winner's Circle on the label to reveal the words "Grand Prize Winner." Then call our toll-free contest hotline at 1-800-555-0707 to claim your two-week, all-expenses-paid dream vacation at Rancho Reductio in exotic Cancun, Mexico.

ALTERNATIVE METHOD OF ENTRY: NO PURCHASE NECESSARY. Using a single $3'' \times 5''$ card, type or legibly print a 3,000-word essay on why you deserve a second honeymoon, with as much explicit, clinical detail as possible on your first honeymoon. A signed note from your personal physician is allowed but not required. Explain exactly what you did or did not find satisfactory the first time around, and why. Don't be shy. Winning (and losing) entries become the sole property of the Econo-Meat Dog Food Company, and may be used in advertisements, promotional campaigns, direct mail offers, billboards, bumper stickers, fast-food action figures, romance novel tie-ins, made-for-TV movies and late-night 900 number commercials. Entries must be received no later than—and no earlier than—midnight, December 31. Econo-Meat Dog Food is not responsible for late, early, damaged or misdirected mail, or for mail intercepted and opened by covert federal agencies, snoopy relatives, passive-aggressive roommates, landladies, or extraterrestrial interlopers. Entrants must be 26 years of age, $5'11''$ tall, weigh 176 pounds, have blond hair and

brown eyes (one on each side of their face), and must have grad-
uated from Wheaton North High School on June 11, 2002. Employees of Econo-Meat Dog Food, El Termino Airlines, and Rancho Reductio and their immediate families are not eligible. Nor
are any members of the species Homo sapiens, or for that matter any erect bipeds, viviparous mammals, vertebrates, or mouth-
breathing creatures located anywhere on the Great Chain of Being. Only one entry per person or personality is allowed. Entrants
suffering from multiple personality syndrome must submit a separate entry for each recognizable psychic entity, and the handwriting must not match. The winner must reside in the 48 con-
tiguous United States, and shall furnish 48 driver's licenses to
prove it. Both legible and illegible entries may be disqualified at
the arbitrary whim of the judges, who reserve the right to pass
sentence of death on any entrant deemed unworthy of winning
or existing. The winner will be selected in a non-random drawing, or "fix," at the headquarters of Econo-Meat Dog Food on or
about October 1. Federal, state and local taxes are the responsibility of the winner, as are any payoffs or bribes necessary to avoid
same. This contest is void where prohibited by law and prohibited
by law where void, whichever comes first. All federal, state and local laws apply—except to the Econo-Meat Dog Food Company, its
heirs, assigns, beneficiaries, business partners or enemies, and
any immediate or distant relatives of its employees, customers
or future litigants. The odds of winning are dependent upon the
number of entries received, in a pig's eye, and may be roughly in-
dicated by a fraction consisting of the numeral "1" over the number of atoms in the known universe. The winner will be notified

by mental telepathy, and will be required to sign an affidavit of eligibility within 24 hours using only the telekinetic power of his or her mind. For a list of winners, send a self-addressed, stamped #10 envelope inside of an unstamped, unaddressed #11 envelope. This precaution will protect your privacy and ours. Prize is subject to flight and hotel availability, with the following blackout dates: January 1 to the Ides of March; March 16 to Independence Day; July 5 to Labor Day; September 2 to Christmas Eve; and December 26 to December 31. Prizes are non-refundable, non-transferable and non-redeemable in cash or any other way. No substitutions by winner. Econo-Meat Dog Food Company reserves the right to substitute a bus ride to Dubuque for the Cancun thing. All meals, taxes, gratuities, air fare and hotel expenses remain the responsibility of the "winner." Room subject to availability and may be replaced by a large cardboard box on a street corner next to a homeless man eating a can of Econo-Meat Dog Food.

Diary of a Radioactive, Flesh-Eating Teen Zombie

September 30

Woke up feeling strange and then gradually understood why: 1) it isn't morning, it's night; 2) someone nearby has been screaming for I don't know how long but it feels, like, foreverish; 3) they're screaming at ME, because 4) as my own bedroom mirror tells me, I've been bitten in the face by a radioactive, flesh-eating zombie, and now I'm one, too. Of course this would have to happen right before Homecoming! And up until now I thought I had a shot at becoming Queen. Oh, well. No use crying over spilt milk—or in this case, buckets of blood and one very loosely hanging eyeball. I don't have a lot of time to ponder this thought as it suddenly dawns on me that the screamer is my geek sister Debbie and I've always wanted to suck her brains out through a straw because she keeps borrowing my lip gloss without asking. Turns out, I don't even need the straw. Ah, peace and quiet at last!

October 1

Realized that being a zombie makes you forget the little things, like how to do stuff without using my teeth. Like this morning, I ran out of my special jasmine-scented hairspray after biting through the aerosol can (which exploded in my face, causing my loose eyeball to dangle down into my bra, kinda gross but kinda cool—I never knew my breasts were this big), so I decided to head over to the salon at the mall. Shuffled slowly with my gory arms outstretched, but I've got to be careful—don't want to overdevelop my deltoids and end up looking like Marcie "I'm-So-Full-of-Myself-'Cause-I'm-School-Wrestling-Champ-and-You're-Not" Penderecki. Note to self: If I see Marcie today I'm going to rip those big arms off and beat her to death with them. She'll be full of herself after I feed her those arms, all right. Wait, gotta stop thinking about food all the time. Why am I so hungry lately? As I say those words to myself I am barely even aware that I've been chewing on the bloody guts of the neighbor's Chihuahua, Taco, who ran up and started barking at me hysterically a minute ago until I bit him in half. Part of me's gonna miss that annoying little guy. But not the part that's digesting him. Mmm-mm.

All at once I feel so guilty. Too much red meat! I have GOT to make myself gulp down a salad at some point, but for some reason all I can think of is brains, brains, fresh, pulsating, delicious raw brains. Nerd alert!

October 4

Never made it to the salon, and let me tell you, Diary, if the rest of the cheerleading squad could see my hair now they'd mock me right off the field. At least until I pulled out their livers with my bare hands. Anyway, the reason I didn't reach the salon is that when I got to the mall I ran into these, well, I guess you could call them "survivors." You know the type: not professional fighters, most of them, but wicked brave and smart and so evenly mixed along racial and gender and socioeconomic lines that your heart just went out to them. Mine did. I could hardly force myself to

143

slice and dice the leader and start snacking on his pancreas. He was hunky. Or, I should say, the hunk of him I managed to swallow was.

One of the others sprayed me with a flamethrower—where'd they find THAT?—and now I've got that horrible charred-flesh smell which makes it so difficult to attract the right flavor of boy. Then they pushed me into a janitor's closet and jammed the door shut, and that's where I've been for three whole days. Boring! Still, the janitor was in here at the time so it hasn't been a total loss. Profound thought: I wonder if people would taste any different if you tore off their greasy gray uniforms BEFORE devouring them? But I must say, his vaguely ammonium seasoning was a nice change of pace from the standard human catch-of-the-day. And with my mild radioactive glow it was almost like having a romantic, candlelit dinner.

October 4 (later the same day)

Two other ghouls burst through the door a while ago, obviously hoping for a live human appetizer. But when they saw it was only little old radioactive, flesh-eating me, they seemed to lose interest and got that listless, mopey, don't-know-who-to-cannibalize-next zombie look in their pale, undead eyes. Losers. I hope nobody thinks I'm with them.

October 4 (still later the same day)

Window-shopped at the shoe outlet until a glance at my own reflection revealed that my left foot is, like, totally GONE and I've been walking on a bloody stump! My mom is so right. I can't keep track of anything anymore. If she heard about this she'd laugh so hard it would kill her (not really—what would kill her would be me chomping and clawing my way through her chest cavity until I yanked the still-beating heart from her body and popped it into my jaws like a gigantic yummy red grape). Mom's sense of humor is really what keeps me going. That and the whole rising-from-the-grave-to-feed-on-your-hot-scrumptious-carcass thing.

October 5

Lonely today. Lonely and blue and hungry. So hungry I chewed a leather hiking boot like a piece of gum just to remind myself of what something that used to be flesh tastes like. For a second, as I was shambling along past the hardware store with one femur poking shamelessly through my jeans (sorry, Mom!), I thought I heard a guy whistle at me. Turns out it was only a Geiger counter. (*Sigh...*)

October 31

Feel like I've been kicked in the head. Or rather, chainsawed in the neck. One of those pesky survivalists must've snuck up behind me with one. I never saw what they looked like because my severed skull has been lying in the same corner of the toy store facing the same baby blue walls for three-and-a-half weeks. I know what you're thinking: "Cutting off a zombie's head kills it." Well, don't believe everything you see in the movies. You probably think there's actually a national treasure, too.

I know what else you're thinking: "How can she be writing this with her head separated from her body?" Hey, don't ask. If I could turn around I might be able to tell you what the rest of me is doing. Let's just say that in a scenario like this, radiation can and does account for almost anything. The worst part is, it didn't even kill my hunger. I mean, yes, I've wanted to lose weight, but not like this! And can someone explain WHY I'm still hungry when I don't even have a stomach anymore? Final thought: What happens now if I give in to irresistible temptation and swallow my own tongue?

OF LOVE

The following essay is excerpted from *50 Card Tricks You Can Do from Beyond the Grave, or Lost Writings of Francis Bacon*. A maelstrom of controversy has surrounded the recently published manuscript, which was claimed to have been discovered by a Chicago butcher, Charles Gorgopopolis, within the entrails of a slaughtered pig.

Since Bacon died in 1626, that would make the pig close to 400 years old, and there are other hints that the book may be apocryphal. In several of the essays the English philosopher refers to his readers as "youse guys" or "regular Joes," and he makes frequent mention of the Sears Tower and microwave ovens. Although the ink was still wet when he brought the pages to the publisher, Gorgopopolis swore they were written by Bacon, or Bacon's wife, or at the very least Shakespeare, or possibly Shakespeare's wife—but definitely someone wearing a goatee.

Authentic or not, the book provides remarkable insight into a man described by some as "a genius for all time," and by others (including the pig) as "a real stinker."

"Love hurteth the heart as a dead mackerel doth offend the nostrils." Thus spake the Greek general Alcibiades after Socrates had utterly refused his advances for that, as the philosopher saith, "They were not cash advances." Indeed, for some, love and money are one, although love doth not pay quarterly dividends. Heracli-

147

tus hath called love, "That which one cannot step in twice without wiping one's sandals." Verily, Heraclitus was an ass.

We may distinguish four varieties of love: the love of parents for their children (when properly seasoned); the love of a boy for his dog; the love between two dogs, a lord chancellor and a bishop in garters; and most wondrous rare, the love between man and wife—so long as it be someone else's wife. One may also speak of the love between a man and a suit of chain mail, but it would be wise to do so in a whisper if there are others present.

Yea, nor should we confound common love with true love. Common love, or as Chaucer hath writ, "a litel on the side, with bosoms," is fit only for beasts and advertising account executives. True love, it will be seen, is always signaled by a rash upon the tongue and abdomen, to which diverse ointments may be applied without relief. If a man feel love for a lady, or even for his wife, he will not dip her hairpiece in a blood pudding or break a 16-piece stoneware dining set upon her brow, although when no one else is looking he may slap her lightly about the face and neck with his broadsword, in jest as it were.

Lastly is the love of heaven and things holy. As Dante hath made note in his crippled rhyme:

"Before mortals would know their Creator's heart,
They first must send candy, or a thank-you card."

Oft hath it been said in truth, Dante was an imbecile, yet he had beautiful handwriting. For God, like the Marines, is looking for a few good men...better men than Tom Cruise, one can but hope. And the love of God will take all good men on a holy pilgrimage, or perhaps a hayride to Hell—the scriptures are not always clear. But if thou shouldst chance to make pilgrimage to Chicago, and if thou hath a taste for fine pork-like killing floor remnants, be sure to pay homage to the Gorgopopolis Sausage Emporium.

MYSTERIES OF AMERICAN HISTORY

One bright summer morning in 1756, in Virginia, a farmer named Emmanuel Boggs rose and stepped—staggered, I should say—over to the window. If he had opened his eyes, he would have seen several hundred acres of prime Virginia tobacco shrouded in dew and stretching like a fine brown mist to the turquoise horizon. But Farmer Boggs was nobody's fool. He kept his eyes good and shut. The last thing a man wants to look at in the morning is miles and miles of tobacco. And in the distance the mad, immortal sea, the cry of the seagull, and the endless lapping of waves on the shore...Farmer Boggs felt a sudden spasm of nausea. Instinctively he put his fist through the glass. He stood gaping at his hand for a while as though it might apologize, and then he went back to bed. He never woke up again, but we mustn't hold that against him. He had taken all that a man could take. The South. Tobacco. A brutal, inhuman system doomed to decline and eventual extinction. Corn whiskey. Gallons of it. And Scarlett, beautiful Scarlett whom he had never met, who would not be born until his son was an old man.

There are other incidents in American history just as puzzling as this one.

In 1833, on a foggy March Thursday, Emil Boggs (no relation) went squirrel hunting in the woods around Natchez, Tennessee. Fifteen minutes later he came back, after realizing he had forgotten his hunting rifle and that he couldn't kill any squirrels by pointing a finger at them, cocking his thumb and yelling "Bang!"

This time he took both his squirrel gun and his dog, whom he called Commander Henry Celsius for reasons that are lost to us, and probably to him, also. Certainly they were lost to the dog, who answered to nothing but "Hey, you!" At any rate, out went Emil, and soon he had shot his quota of squirrels. Before long he had shot double his quota, and then triple. He had also shot his wife, his brother, a man who looked like his brother, a man who looked like his wife, and a man who looked like Teddy Roosevelt, although Roosevelt would not be born for another 25 years. He just didn't know *how* to quit. The local constables grilled him for hours, but when asked why he had shot all those people he would only reply, "Because they had big, bushy tails and scampered from tree to tree." It was an airtight alibi. Reluctantly, they let him go.

Two years later to the day, he was found floating face down in the reservoir, and such was the esteem the townspeople had for him that no one bothered to pull him out, although they did put up a "No Swimming" sign. Commander Henry Celsius changed his name to Emiliano Zapata (no relation) and moved to Mexico, where he was to write his memoirs and cause no end of confusion.

In October, 1928, Emily Boggs (again, no relation), who worked as a silkworm in a New York textile plant, passed out of human ken for three days. For 72 hours no one knew where she was, and what's more, no one cared. When she finally returned to work she was wearing a false mustache, and her breath left something to be desired. She waved a loaded revolver in the air, or vice versa, and declared in a rotten Spanish accent: "I am Emiliano Zapata. Put your hands up and don't lower them until I say 'Simon Says.' " Nobody noticed, as it was a Sunday and the plant was closed. After several minutes of indecision she fell north-by-northwest into a bucket of boiling tar, muttering some words that were either poor English or very poor Spanish. Five days later she was arrested in Salt Pork, Oregon, for writing out checks in Roman numerals and making some grave errors in arithmetic. She was taken in with a tall, bearded man who called himself Abraham Lincoln, although Lincoln had been killed 63 years previously. The Birth of the Blues would not come for another four years.

On a hot Sunday night not long ago, the author of this article (no relation, but I know him pretty well and he's a really sweet guy) glanced up from his work to find that it was 10:15, more than two hours past his bedtime. He was tired, so very tired. The Birth of a Nation was already more than 200 years in the past. There was no point in sending a greeting card now. He tiptoed off to bed so as not to awaken the guard dog.

MONKA BUSINESS

*A federal jury in Reno, Nevada, has returned a verdict of innocent in the
case of a bank robbery suspect who is said to have three personalities, one
of them an observer from another world. Under questioning by his attorney,
Jack Paul Faulkner, 52, displayed his three personalities, Jack, Paul, and
Monka. Monka told the jury: "I am the spirit who at one time was flesh who
now does not reside on your planet. I am an observer only." Faulkner main-
tained he "couldn't and wouldn't rob a bank."*—Actual newspaper clip-
ping found among my father's papers, though the name of the
newspaper and the date of the story are now lost to time

I append the above news item for those with a casual interest in the doings of their neighbors from another world. Several
questions in regard to this article, not all of them legal in nature,
keep nagging at me.

Just for starters, I am puzzled as to how and why the jury (a
federal jury, mind you) returned a verdict of innocent for Mr. Jack
Paul "Monka" Faulkner. On the face of it, you'd think that a man
possessing three personalities, or even four or five, would be every bit as capable of bank robbing as you or I. My three dozen personalities would never keep me from a life of crime if I thought I
could arrange to have all of my trials held in Reno, Nevada.

Then there is the problem of "Monka," as he sees fit to call
himself. I don't doubt that there is a Monka, or that he is from
another world. Neither do I doubt that he was tried by a jury of
his peers; by which I mean that any jury that could acquit Monka
on the alibi he gives is definitely from another world, unquestion-

ably a place where oysters run for president and banks leave their vaults unlocked for creatures with three or more personalities to rifle through the assets.

Why must we so frequently assume that our extraterrestrial neighbors are not only further advanced than us scientifically (*that* I can accept), but also infinitely kinder, more benevolent, harmless, and, if you'll pardon the expression, more humane? In our naïve fantasies we picture them coming to Earth simply for the amusement provided by the human spectacle, or to bestow upon us a gadget that will end all war and tell us which horses are good in the fifth race at Aqueduct besides. Apart from those made-for-TV movies on the SyFy channel, the typical alien is, for most of us, a sort of intellectual Tony Robbins.

My guess is that any race of beings that can find its way to what Alfred Whitehead called a "second-rate planet with a second-rate star" is looking for some easy swag, and what's more has the means to get it. Their scientists, nothing but a pack of interstellar hoodlums, are sweating right now over the plans for a device that will pop open every safe deposit box in the world, while simultaneously immobilizing every teller and permitting unruly monsters with three nasty personalities to loot to their heart's content, if they *have* hearts. I'll bet they have three apiece, the scum!

But that way lies delirium. Let us not presume the worst about Monka's people, whatever we may think of him personally. Let us merely induce that Monka is a finger man for a small but vile band of galactic pirates, working hand-in-glove with his earthly cronies, those traitors to the human race Jack and Paul. He offered these two Benedict Arnolds a tempting reward, say, a date with a nice set of personalities or a seat on the federal bench in Reno, Nevada, and for such a trifle they sold out their fellow men and gave Monka houseroom in the body of Mr. Faulkner, the better to execute his cold-blooded schemes.

I won't be taken in by that mushy double-talk of his. "An observer only"—hah! He was casing the joint, that's all. Any two-bit private detective could tell you as much. And as for that other bit of buncombe, the one that goes "I am the spirit who at one time was flesh who now does not reside on your planet"—well, the jury that fell for *that* one ought to be strapped down under a strobe light and forced to read the collected works of Mary Baker Eddy. What does he mean, "who at one time was flesh"? If a 52-year-old man doesn't have flesh on him he's on the wrong side of the ground and they might as well hang him because he wouldn't notice the difference. And if he doesn't reside on our planet, how does he come to be in a court of law? He saw fit to hire an attorney, didn't he? After all, Jack and Paul couldn't and wouldn't take that kind of initiative. That's evidence enough for me.

The lone alternative to believing that the men and women of the jury are hallucinating is that they are shielding someone, namely Jack and Paul. They feel that their compatriots have been bedazzled by a visitor from the starry heavens, innocently beguiled into helping Monka pull off his heist. Jack and Paul thought it was all in good fun, or so this gullible jury would have us believe. Let me tell you, when personalities named Monka appear out of nowhere demanding a piece of the action, innocent men, even schizoids, don't stick around to listen. They put their fingers in their ears and shriek until the ambulance comes.

The whole business has the air of a carnival sideshow. "Faulkner *displayed* his three personalities," the item reads (my italics). Display is for kindergartners at show-and-tell. Or performance artists. Or strippers. It has no place in American jurisprudence. Faulkner sounds like a regular Alfred E. Neuman the way he lets Monka, not to mention Jack and Paul, play him for a fool. Such things may be a matter of course in Reno, but I, for one, am disquieted by the precedent seemingly set by this case. Let us pray that if vaudeville ever does return it confines itself to the stage and leaves the courtroom to sober people with only one personality.

Come to think of it, if multiple personalities are to be recognized in a court of law, why shouldn't each of the body-sharing defendants be charged, tried and sentenced separately? Actually, that might work— and I could serve on three dozen juries at once!

Art Is a Concept by Which We Measure Our Pain

The first time I saw Ted Grundelman, he was popping yellow 25-watt light bulbs into his mouth, chewing them thoroughly and spitting the pieces into a red wastepaper basket labeled "People's Republic of China." This was at a retrospective of his work at the Museum of Contemporary Art. This particular piece ("Untitled Number Nine") concluded with Ted asking someone in the audience for a drink of water, at which point he would break the glass with a ball-peen hammer while reciting the Periodic Table of Elements in that deeply resonant yet strangely tender voice of his.

It was, quite simply, a revelation. I had never seen a conceptual artist before, and Ted was somehow more than an artist—he *became* his work; he was Art itself. I knew I must speak to him. I pressed in among the crowd of admirers in time to discover Ted's uncompromising way of giving autographs. He would jab his wrist with a fine-point pen and sign, with his own blood, "putty-head Picasso" or "that maggot Monet." I could contain myself no longer.

"M-Mr. Grundelman," I stammered. He turned on me in a white-faced fury.

"What did you call me?" he hissed, waving a switchblade in one hand and advancing on me with amazing swiftness.

"I'm sorry, Ted, I mean Mr. Grundelman, I—" His features softened suddenly.

"That's more like it," he said, as he put the switchblade into the leg of the man standing next to him. "Now, what can I do for you?"

"I don't want your autograph," I began.

"That makes two of us," he said.

"I want to know more about you," I continued. "Can we talk?"

"I don't know. Can we?" He smiled. He had a secret way of putting you at ease. I remember thinking, This man will be my friend for life. We ended up a few doors down at a little place called Plato's Cave. Ted was drinking Hemlock Manhattans as if there were no tomorrow, pausing only to toss off sweeping evaluations of other artists, living and dead: "Rembrandt? Rembrandt couldn't paint his way out of a box of Kleenex. Van Gogh should have cut off *both* his ears. My grandmother paints better than Salvador Dali, and she's been dead for 20 years." He held me spellbound.

"When did you first think of yourself as an artist?" I asked him. A strange, brooding darkness clouded his eyes. He looked down at his drink.

"You know those ads in the back of *Guns and Ammo* magazine, 'Draw the leprechaun and win a $500 art scholarship'?" I nodded. "Well, I drew the leprechaun, but I didn't win any scholarship." By now his voice was trembling. "I didn't win a goddamned pencil!" he shouted, and in the same instant threw his mug at the head of a total stranger, killing the fellow before he hit the floor. I paid for the mug and left a big tip. With Ted tagging at my heels calling me "the Whore of Babylon" and "a filthy Philistine," I managed to hail a cab and deliver him home, which was nothing but an abandoned abattoir by the railroad yards.

Over the next few months I watched Grundelman's career rise, peak and then plummet to its tragic finish. His works became outlandishly daring. For one exhibit at the Guggenheim Museum he had a meat locker installed in the main wing, then he shut himself inside with 12 go-go dancers, a closed-circuit TV camera and a 100-gallon tub of steak sauce. When he emerged several weeks later Modern Art was forever changed—and so was he. He had a haunted look about him. He kept glancing over his shoulder to make sure he wasn't being followed by store mannequins, which of course he was.

His next one-man show had him juggling three live tarantulas while dipping his bare feet into some sour cream. The *New York Times* called it "a terrible waste of good sour cream... not the kind of thing you want hanging over the fireplace." For a while, out of sheer despair, Ted switched to oil-on-velvet portraits of conquistadors, but his own self-destructive vision finally caught up with him. The end was near. He bought a cheap pine coffin and painted a huge yellow smiley face on the outside. After lining the interior with corn plasters and bay leaves, he lay down in it and locked the lid from the inside. He took nothing with him but some pistachio nuts. My review of this, his masterpiece, was to be our final farewell:

"There is a strength, a stubbornness in the lines of Grundelman's new work that says he knows where he's going, and he isn't coming back. He suffered to show us ourselves. May he rest wherever he is.

"But at least he could have left us some pistachio nuts."

THE SPIRIT OF CHRISTMAS

My Dear Mr. Vanderwoude,

Thank you for your recent gift. Now once again as the holidays approach we ask you to remember the plight of the Bosnian and Serbian orphans. For many of these children there will be no Christmas—no presents, no toys, and worst of all no parents to love and protect them. We thank you for your past generosity and hope you will not forget these little ones as you enjoy the comfort and affluence of your safe, warm home during this joyous season.

Yours sincerely,

Kurt Luchs

P.S. Please accept the enclosed paper Christmas wreath, hand-constructed by seven-year-old burn victim Susie, and hang it on your tree. I trust you'll think of the orphans whenever you look at it.

※ ※ ※ ※ ※

Dear Mr. Vanderwoude,

If this letter happens to cross yours in the mail, please forgive me; I know the post office is slow and unreliable during the Christmas rush. I'm sure you received my last letter and that your generous gift is already on its way to help the homeless orphans of war-torn Bosnia-Herzegovina. But just in case our letter—or even yours, God forbid—might have gone astray, I'm sending this reminder to thank you for what you have already done and to ask if you can find it in your heart to do just a little bit more this Christmas.

Yours sincerely,

Kurt Luchs

P.S. The attached miniature pinecone, painted holiday green and dipped in glitter, was brought back from the former war zone in the tattered coat pocket of a little boy we call Buster. Enjoy.

✻ ✻ ✻ ✻ ✻

Dear Mr. Vanderwoude,

I'll admit I'm puzzled. Surely you must have received my previous letters asking you to add just a little holiday cheer to the lives of our orphaned Bosnian and Serbian boys and girls. And surely you cannot be unmoved by their tragic plight—after all, you made a significant contribution to our cause only a few months ago. Perhaps you yourself have faced unfortunate circumstances recently—a long illness, the loss of a job, or even the loss of a loved one. If so, I offer you my deepest, most heartfelt sympathy, and I look forward to hearing from you in the near future when things are going better for you.

But if you are not facing hard times, Mr. Vanderwoude, if what you suffer from is merely a hard heart... God help you, Mr. Vanderwoude.

Yours,

Kurt Luchs

P.S. The enclosed sketch of the dove of peace was done by little Amalric, a paraplegic war orphan who has learned to draw by holding a piece of charcoal between his teeth. I hope it fills you with the generous spirit of Christmas.

* * * * *

Mr. Vanderwoude,

As I write this, the orphans are weeping. I had to tell them that there would be no toys this Christmas, that they might not even have a roof over their heads come December 25th. "Why?" they cried. "Because a man named Richard Vanderwoude has apparently decided that your unimaginable pain doesn't matter," I said. "Because he has put his own selfish whims and desires above your basic needs. Because he thinks you are not worth saving." At that point I had to restrain one of the children, Tedescu, from leaping through a plate-glass window.

How can I be so sure of your lack of charity? You see, Mr. Vanderwoude, I did a little checking around. I found that you are not sick, that none of your friends or loved ones have died recently, and that you have not only not been fired but have received a substantial raise and promotion in the past few months.

I am not enclosing a postpaid return envelope with this letter because if you do decide to melt your icy heart and send a donation (which I doubt), I think it appropriate that you should pick up the tab.

Yours,

Kurt Luchs

P.S. The enclosed finger painting portrait of you (you're the one with the fangs) is by Lisel, an eight-year-old deaf-mute. The bright object underneath you is either a holiday candle or the flames of Hell. Of course we can't ask Lisel, can we?

❊ ❊ ❊ ❊ ❊

Mr. Vanderwoude,

If you think you can escape the consequences of your evil actions (or rather, inactions) you are wrong. You will pay. I will see to it personally. And I'll have lots of help. You forget, Mr. Vanderwoude, that these are Bosnian and Serbian orphans. They have been handling firearms and explosives since they were two. They are really pissed off at the world and don't know who to blame, but you make a very plausible target. We know where you live.

Kurt Luchs

P.S. The fiery red composition I've attached to this letter is the joint effort of Tommy and Tony, identical twins who have sworn a sacred blood oath (that's their blood on the paper) not to rest until they have taken vengeance upon you. The artwork depicts your head as it would look after a losing encounter with a fragmentation grenade—a picture I hope to see someday in real life.

❊ ❊ ❊ ❊ ❊

O Ricky boy,

You've really done it now, mister. I heard the cops coming up the stairs and managed to hide in an air vent while they ransacked my office. After they left I took the few weapons they had missed, stuffed my remaining files into a briefcase and then torched the place.

So now you know there are no orphans—Bosnian, Serbian, or Martian. But that doesn't let you off the hook, Rick. Not by a long shot. If there had been any orphans, they would have been just as hungry and hopeless as my letters made out, and you'd be just as guilty. Oh no, Vanderwoude, you aren't out of the woods yet. Because no matter where you go or how much police protection they give your worthless ass, I'll find you, I'll hunt you down like a dog and show you ethnic cleansing like you've never seen before.

If I were you I'd start drinking gallon jugs of double espresso right now and make plans to never, ever go to sleep again. Better install rearview mirrors on your glasses, too. Wherever you are, I'll be right behind you.

Kurt Luchs

P.S. Enclosed is an artist's rendering of the place I'd most like to visit on this earth: your grave.

Muzak of the Spheres, or: What is the Sound of One Woody Allen Clapping?

(An excerpt from Volume 56 in the Collected Works *of the iconoclastic philosopher Allan Stewart Konigsberg.)*

Let me say at the outset of my treatise that I am interested only in the ultimate questions: Is there a God? Did He create the universe, or did He buy it ready-made from one of the better mail-order houses? How do we know what we know, and if we don't know, how can we fake it? What is morality, and why do all the girls I meet seem to have it? What is man? What is woman? And why don't they ever sign their real names on the register?

These are not idle questions, but a matter of life and death. I'm locking the door right now, and if one of us doesn't come up with the answers within the next ten minutes then both of us will die. Since I am a fictional character, I assure you this will be much harder on you than on me.

Philosophy begins with metaphysics, and as Kant was fond of saying to his mirror, "I never metaphysics I didn't like." This cryptic comment becomes much clearer when we consider that Kant was a boob—what's more, a boob with a speech impediment. He would say "categorical imperative" when what he really wanted was a hamburger and fries. Nor was Spinoza any closer to the truth when he defined the will as a thing-in-itself. The thing-in-itself was his wife, who divorced him for demonstrating the principle of Universal Love by giving a rubdown to a rabbi. It was

Spinoza, however, who, in a brilliant paper on optics, proved that a magnifying glass could be used to commit arson.

Throughout the ages, great thinkers have gone beyond the conventional wisdom to seek the inner meaning of life. Nietzsche went *Beyond Good and Evil;* B. F. Skinner went *Beyond Freedom and Dignity;* Russ Meyer went *Beyond the Valley of the Dolls.* These three profoundly different geniuses have one thing in common: they will never become championship bowlers. Yet their ideas will live forever, or at least until they are made into Broadway musicals.

"What is truth?" asked jesting Pilate, and would not stay for an answer (though he did watch it later on Blu-ray). I define truth as that which should never be uttered before a subcommittee or a microphone. Further, true Being is distinguishable from being in Gary, Indiana— especially if you try to breathe.

If God exists then human life makes sense (with the exception of Suge Knight); if God does not exist then everything is meaningless, and there's no point making good on those gambling debts.

Some radical theologians claim that God is dead, while others insist He's just "resting His eyes." Either way, He's not taking any calls. The Bible tells us He is an angry God and a jealous God— character traits the BBC might keep in mind the next time they're casting *Othello.*

God or no, all rational beings, and even Unitarians, must eventually confront the problem of good and evil. Those sufficiently enlightened choose the good, but many elect to go into real estate instead. What dark mystery of the soul causes one person to abandon wickedness for a life of sainthood, and another to become a Top 40 radio programmer?

For that matter, how can we tell that we actually exist, that we are not mere phantoms? Of course *I* am—as I said, I'm only a mythical mouthpiece for a sick mind—but what about you? Are you too, perhaps, an invented character with fictitious needs and desires and cold sores created by a demented writer? If I stopped talking to you would you simply disappear? And if so, could the same method be applied to a Jehovah's Witness?

Conversely, if you stopped reading this would I vanish? Most importantly, would the author still get his check?

The Imperturbable Mrs. Luchs

Do not judge my mother.

You don't get to do that unless you go and have seven children, one right after the other, in just ten years. Pretty much everything strange and mystifying about her mothering could be ascribed to a never-ending case of postpartum depression. And that's before you take a closer look at those children. If you want to know what kind of feral society we siblings formed in the absence of real adult supervision, reread *The Lord of the Flies*.

Even if you do happen to have popped out seven unruly mini-monsters in one decade, you still don't get to judge her because you were not married to my father, a maxi-monster if ever there was one—and there was. Dad was an ex-Marine, which is like being an ex-Catholic: i.e., there is no such thing, because once they have you, they have you for life, run where you will. He taught us the words to "The Halls of Montezuma" (a.k.a. "The Marine Corps Hymn") before any other song, even Christmas carols, though for reasons best known to himself he often made us sing it while goose-stepping and delivering the Nazi salute. Come to think of it, he had us sing Christmas carols the same way. Under his command, we didn't merely clean the yard, we *policed* the yard. Yes, yard maintenance was a police action like the Korean War, in which he had served as a sharpshooter, and about which he never uttered one syllable to me or, to my knowledge, to any of my siblings. He made the Great Santini look like Gomer Pyle.

But I am getting away from the subject, which is supposed to be my mother. Perhaps partly in reaction to my father's short fuse, profane vocabulary and lethal military training, she cultivated a persona resembling that of Blanche DuBois in *A Streetcar Named Desire*. She lived in a world of her own. It was a world more like Rivendell than planet Earth, populated by fairies and elves and myths and mythters, not by Stanley Kowalski's understudy and seven hell-spawn. Inhabiting this mystic mental fog may have been what preserved any sanity she had left. She could retreat into it at will, and did so constantly. It made her unflappable and imperturbable, and as we shall see at certain crucial moments, utterly unreachable.

She read poetry. Worse, she wrote it. Some of my earliest and most persistent childhood memories are of her drifting through the house iambically reciting Yeats, Frost, Eliot and Dylan Thomas aloud. That kind of thing gets into a boy's head. It would be many years before I understood that other mothers, normal mothers, did not carry on so. She also knew by heart many songs by the Irish folk sensations The Clancy Brothers, such as "The Wild Colonial Boy," "Whiskey You're the Devil," and "The Men of the West." Her renditions were seldom on key, but gained in power when our two dogs and half dozen cats caught the spirit of it and added their own howls to the choruses.

Speaking of animals, her big heart for them was the reason our house and yard on the outskirts of pristine, suburban Wheaton, Illinois, looked more like a Dust Bowl farm. In addition to the dogs and an unending supply of cats and kittens, we had four chickens and four geese, along with an occasional hamster or mouse and any number of woodland creatures that we rescued (usually from our own cats) and kept temporarily until we could turn them over to the Willowbrook Wildlife Center. These included everything from bats and raccoons to pheasants and opossums. We had a pet crow named Edgar Allan Crow, whom we taught to say, among other things, "Nevermore" and "Brookwillow" (his charmingly dyslexic attempt at "Willowbrook"). Imitating our mother with cruel accuracy, he could also scream, "Shut the door!" and do a very moving impersonation of a baby crying, one of the few ways to get her attention.

For some reason it was the men of the family who brought home the amphibians and reptiles. I kept a newt and a small tortoise, and usually an aquarium stocked with painted turtles and crayfish. One winter I housed twenty-seven baby snapping turtles in an aluminum tub under the kitchen sink. Why? I don't know. Maybe I was taken with their hypnotic little six-pointed starry eyes and the fact that at that tender age, their vicious bites couldn't even break the skin. It is a testament of sorts to my mother's culinary skills that the smell of those turtles and whatever she was cooking could not easily be distinguished. It is a testament to her imperturbability that she allowed them to remain in the kitchen all winter with the windows shut tight against the Northern Illinois cold.

My father topped us all when he and a Marine Corps buddy returned from a fossil hunting trip in the western part of the state with a live timber rattlesnake. Not many women would have retained their composure under the circumstances. My mother was delighted, almost giddy. She promptly named the snake Gertrude and put her in a Plexiglas cage in the crawlspace. Gertrude proved very useful while we had her. When we caught some of the neighbor kids trying to steal our bicycles, we showed them Gertrude. We urged them to make sudden movements in front of her cage, causing her to strike at the Plexiglas. The venom from her fangs dripped down the inside of her cage quite dramatically. We never had to lock up our bikes again. Eventually we donated Gertrude to the Brookfield Zoo. Six months later she was killed by a falling rock under suspicious circumstances, and I believe the Chicago Police Department may still have a cold case file on her. My mother wore a black armband for a year.

I've told you about the good times, the times when Mom's imperturbability was an asset to a household full of wild creatures, human and otherwise. But there were other times, too. Times when her ability to retreat into those golden mental mists almost amounted to neglect. Again, I ask you not to judge. You weren't there. You can't know what it was like. You probably think I'm exaggerating or inventing for comic effect, but you have no idea how wrong you are, or how much I'm actually leaving out because you would never believe it.

Take the time when I nearly bled out on the living room couch while she sat there reading the paper. The evening had started normally enough. I always had a copious supply of fireworks around, which I needed for my ongoing scientific and philanthropic work. That night I was working with bottle rockets. I had become jaded with the pedestrian experience of setting them off one at a time. Inspired by the twin ideas of a Roman candle and a Gatling gun, I used corrugated cardboard to construct a multiple bottle rocket launcher. It was fiendishly simple. Roll the cardboard into a tube, and stick a bottle rocket into each of the many holes at the end. Then twist all of the fuses together, light them simultaneously, aim the tube at your target, and *voilà*! Instant hellfire.

In this case my target was a Wheaton Police cruiser. There was an intersection nearby with a small hill overlooking it. Perched behind the crest of that hill, I waited until the cruiser stopped at the empty intersection and then set off my launcher. Seconds later, dozens of bottle rockets zipped and whistled and exploded over the cruiser's windshield. I'm sure the two patrolmen, who had probably never handled anything more menacing than a kitten in a tree, thought they had somehow found themselves in the middle of a gang war in sedate, lily-white Wheaton. Within moments, though, they figured it out. Their siren and cherries went on, and they began flashing their searchlight around the car, looking for a criminal mastermind.

I ducked and quickly rolled back down the hill. On the way down, my right calf encountered one of those beer cans from the days before pop tops, the type you had to open with a can opener, leaving a protruding jagged metallic triangle that could do real damage. It ripped through my jeans and opened a gash several inches long in my leg, which began bleeding profusely. A sizable, grisly-looking piece of flesh dangled by a thread. Not having the time or the means to apply a field dressing, I hightailed it home through empty lots overgrown with weeds, keeping as close to the ground as possible.

I burst through the front door out of breath, and haltingly told Mom that I had been injured and would require medical attention. I also mentioned that we needed to turn off the lights and draw the curtains, and if the police came to the door, we should pretend not to be home. "Oh no you don't," she said, without even looking up from her newspaper. "I'm not going to fall for that again."

Perhaps I should explain here that only the previous day I had conducted a different experiment, wherein I combined ashes, candle wax and ketchup into a fair imitation of a horrific burn wound on my left arm. That had got her to take notice, however briefly. But actions have consequences.

Not knowing what else to do, I sat down and let my cut bleed onto the floor. I began to get dizzy, whether from shock and adrenaline or loss of blood, I don't know. The cop car slowly pulled down our cul-de-sac and back out again without stopping, gumballs still on but siren off. A few minutes later my mom finally put down the paper, looked up, saw the growing pool of blood at my feet, and smiled. "Well, are you going to clean that up, or what?" she asked. I managed to whisper that I needed to see a doctor, the sooner the better. Then I fainted.

When at last she understood that I was indeed hurt, she calmly and coolly snapped into action. She had the neighbors drive me to the emergency room. Dad was not home, you see, and she would not learn to drive until many years later. In fact, most pedestrians and light poles unlucky enough to find themselves in her path would say she never did. But that's another story.

The wound took thirty-three stitches to close. The scar is still visible today. As usual, though, there were compensations. The respect of my peers, for one thing. Drugs, for another. That was back when they handed out opiates like Veteran's Day poppies, even to children. It would be several more years before I would test Mom's patience to the limit by starting a hydroponic marijuana farm in the basement and using my augmented chemistry set to synthesize mescaline in honor of Aldous Huxley, another author to whom she introduced me. For now, I was satisfied to have gotten a rise out of two imperturbable entities, the Wheaton Police and Mom, with Mom being by far the tougher nut to crack.

HEADS UP: TOP HEADLINES OF THE 20TH & 21ST CENTURIES

(This piece was originally published in Slate in 1999 as a harbinger of the new millennium. In preparing it for this volume I took the liberty of editing it slightly and expanding it greatly to include more jokes all around, as well as some headlines from the 21st century. There are now two Taft jokes, can you believe it? Although it is fake news, it has no connection to the best-known purveyor of fake news, for whom I used to work. I include it here because it represents the only such material of mine that I have the legal right to reprint. And because I think it's fun.)

Near-Sighted Teddy Roosevelt Bags President McKinley On Safari	*1901*
Wright Brothers Announce 3-Second Meal Service On All 12-Second Flights	*1903*
President Taft Calls For Federal Legislation To Enlarge Doorways, Railway Seats, Bathtubs	*1908*
Albania Lapses Into Anarchy 85 Years Too Soon	*1912*
Shipping Magnate Declares *Titanic*-Iceberg Merger Successful	*1912*
Congress Creates IRS "To Unite Nation Against Common Enemy"	*1913*
Panama Canal Opens New Era Of Global Trade In Panama Hats	*1914*

1914   Fighting Breaks Out Between War Correspondents

1915   German Submarine Fires Warning Torpedo Into *Lusitania*

1916   Army Physicians Laud Mustard Gas As First Inhalable Condiment

1917   President Wilson Promises To Make World Safe For World Wars

1918   Lenin Orders Pictures Of Czar's Family Put On Milk Cartons

1918   Wife's Honeymoon Antics Give Gandhi Idea Of Passive Resistance

1919   Congress Votes For Prohibition, Celebrates With First Toast In Congressional Speakeasy

1919   Senate Rejects Treaty Of Versailles For Having Suspicious Foreign-Sounding Name

1920   Women Experience Futility Of Voting Firsthand

1920   Newly Formed ACLU Vows To Fight Wonderful Laws "Just Because We're Assholes"

1921   Humane Loophole In Immigration Quotas Lets Some Foreigners Enter U.S. As Livestock

1925   Heisenberg Says Uncertainty Principle May Or May Not Be Greatest Discovery Ever

1927   Parisian Hijacker Forces Charles Lindbergh To Make Nonstop Transatlantic Flight at Gunpoint

Supreme Court Rules Films Do Not Have Right To Remain Silent — *1927*

Babe Ruth Seldom Gets To First, Admits Wife — *1928*

Stock Market Crashes When Janet Yellin's Time Machine Crashes Into Stock Market — *1929*

Al Capone Denies Murder For Profit Allegations, Insists Gangland Slayings "Purely For Fun" — *1929*

Taft's Coffin Rapidly Approaching Center Of Earth — *1930*

Hobo Tycoon Announces Plan To Merge With Plate Of Beans — *1930*

Germany Begins Peaceful, Orderly Transition To Totalitarian Madness — *1933*

U.S. Goes Off Gold Standard, Adopts Moldy Crust Of Bread Standard — *1933*

FDR's "The Only Thing We Have To Fear Is Eleanor" Speech Calms Nation — *1933*

New Deal, Same Deck — *1933*

First Woman Cabinet Member, Frances Perkins, Celebrates By Getting Coffee For Other Cabinet Members — *1933*

Newborn Ralph Nader Files Suit Against Mother For Ejecting Him Into Hostile, Unsafe Environment — *1934*

1935   Alcoholics Anonymous Sells First Mailing List To Smirnoff

1935   National Labor Relations Act Recognizes Workers' Right To Be Fired Collectively

1935   Remaining Chinese Communists Receive "I Survived The Long March" T-Shirts

1936   Moscow Show Trials Notably Lacking in Good Show Tunes

1936   Spanish Civil War Erupts As Bullfighters, Flamenco Dancers Clash Over Limited Supply Of Tights

1936   Germany Begins Rearming "Just In Case Those Trigger-Happy Swiss Go Nuts On Us"

1937   Jobless Rate Tops 110 Percent With Many Unemployed At More Than One Occupation

1937   Over-Excited Hindenburg Announcer Explodes

1938   Chamberlain Calls Hitler "The Nicest Totalitarian Madman I've Ever Appeased"

1939   Poland Invades Itself

1940   Millions Of Women Enter Workforce For Lower Pay, Longer Hours; "It's The Greatest Thing Since Slavery!" Say Industry Leaders

1940   Leon Trotsky Dies In First Ice-Pick-Assisted Suicide

"Neither A Borrower Nor A Lender Be" Clause Added To Lend-Lease Act *1941*

Japanese Stir-Fry Pearl Harbor *1941*

French Resistance Waiters Bravely Refuse To Refill Nazi Officers' Coffee Cups *1942*

Discoverer Of LSD Saved From Madness By Absence Of Pink Floyd Records *1943*

Oklahoma! Admitted To Union; Sprightly Musical To Replace Boring Actual State *1943*

Allied Soldiers Hear Of Nude French Sunbathing, Storm Normandy Beaches *1944*

G.I. Bill Guarantees Vets A Lonely, Lingering Death In A Dirty V.A. Hospital *1944*

German V-8 Rockets Splatter London With Delicious, Vitamin-Enriched Tomato Juice *1944*

Stalin "Genuinely Touched" By Gift Of Eastern Europe At Potsdam Surprise Party *1945*

New Volkswagen Requires Ethnically Pure Gasoline *1945*

FAA Charges Drunken UFO Pilot In Roswell Crash *1947*

Truman Defeats Dewey; Huey And Louie Have Yet To Concede *1948*

NATO To Defend West Against Hostile Acronyms *1949*

1950   U.S. Blamed For Starting Hopeless Asian Land War 15 Years Too Soon

1951   Tibetan Puppet Government Charms The Children Of Tibet

1951   President Limited To Two Terms, Two Mistresses

1953   Physicist Murray Gell-Mann Discovers Certain Particles, Brother-In-Law, Have Property Of "Strangeness"

1954   Some TV Couples May Be Sleeping Together, Say Insiders

1956   U.S.S.R. Asks Hungary If It Has Parking Spaces For 10,000 Tanks

1956   Thousands Of Innocent Soviet Corpses Thrilled By Posthumous Rehabilitation

1958   First Hospice Allows Patients To Die In Homelike Setting—Surrounded by Greedy, Hateful Relatives

1959   Congressional Quiz Show Investigators Stunned By Revelation That Not Everything On TV Is Real

1959   Flag-Manufacturing Lobbyists Succeed In Getting Alaska, Hawaii Admitted To Union

1960   U-2 Shot Down Over U.S.S.R.; Infant Bono Unhurt

1960   Emily Post Excuses Self from Table, Dies

Birth Control Pill Replaces Unbearable Ugliness As Main Method Of Contraception *1960*

JFK's Affirmative Action Law Based On Novel Idea That Two Wrongs Make A Right *1961*

CIA Markets Bay Of Pigs Blooper Reel *1961*

Civil War In Yemen Alerts World To Existence Of Yemen *1962*

Folksinger Demands To Know Current Location Of Flowers *1962*

Thousands Of Innocent Trees Die To Make *Silent Spring* A Best Seller *1962*

JFK Accidentally Struck Down By Flying Zapruder Lens Cap *1963*

Rockefellers, Kennedys Conscientiously Object To War On Poverty *1964*

Sensitive Youth Conscientiously Objects To Having Nuts Blown Off In Vietnam *1965*

Marshall McLuhan Caught Reading *1966*

Robert McNamara Commended By PTA for Applying New Math To U.S. Casualty Figures *1966*

Sinatra Shelves Album Of Hendrix Covers *1967*

Martin Luther King Jr., RFK Assassinated Separately But Equally *1968*

1968   Hippies, Beatniks Sign Historic Personal Hygiene Ban

1968   Nonproliferation Treaty Strictly Limits Nuclear Weapons To Nations That Can Afford Them

1968   Kerner Commission Attributes Watts Riots To "Crazy-Ass Muthafuckas"

1968   *Whole Earth Catalog* Temporarily Out Of Stock Of Whole Earths

1969   Teddy Kennedy Charged With "Leaving The Scene Of A Successful Cover-Up"

1970   Near-Perfect Neil Young Guitar Solo Ruined By Addition Of Second Note

1972   J. Edgar Hoover Buried In Simple But Elegant Black Dress

1973   Liz Taylor Will Use New Bar Code Technology To Track Husbands

1973   Entire Consumer Product Safety Commission Dies In Pinto Explosion

1974   Ford Pardons Nixon For Plaid Trousers

1974   Good News: Smelly Ozone Layer Disappearing

1977   IBM Monopoly Threatens Free Market, Warns Head Of Tiny Start-Up Microsoft

1979   U.S. Embassy In Iran Under New Management

MTV Brings Western Civilization To Official Halt	*1981*
Reagan Shot En Route To NRA Fund-Raiser	*1981*
Sandra Day O'Connor Receives Congratulatory Pat On The Behind From Fellow Justices	*1981*
Sweden Attempts To Conserve Remaining Supply Of ABBA	*1982*
First Man With Artificial Heart Has First Artificial Heart Attack	*1983*
"Mondale Fever" Sweeps Minnesota, District Of Columbia	*1984*
"We Are The World" Gives Hope To Rock Has-Beens Starving For A Hit	*1985*
Ollie North Wins Daytime Emmy	*1987*
Democratic Platform Not High Enough To Make Dukakis Visible	*1988*
Chinese Authorities Kick Off "Keep Tiananmen Square Clean" Week With Special Tank Sweepers	*1989*
Scientist Achieves Cold Fusion On Honeymoon	*1989*
Iraqi Army Stages Spirited 3/8-Of-A-Second Counteroffensive	*1991*

1993   Fish And Wildlife Service Reports Whooping Cranes, Young Republicans Breeding In Captivity

1994   Abstinence TV Spots Boost Teen Celibacy To A Record 0.0002 percent

1996   Desperate Postmaster General Tries To Hand-deliver E-Mail

1997   AOL Offers 50 Hours Of Free Downtime

1998   Wave Of 1970s Nostalgia Drives Up Oil Prices

1998   Primitive Amazon Tribe Still Using Apple IIs

1999   China's Abacuses Still Reeling From Year 2000 B.C. Problem

2000   Internet Fills Up Last 3 Percent Of Terrifying Void Of Existence

2001   ACLU Targets Lactose Intolerance

2002   Harvard To Accept Mortal Kombat Scores In Place Of SATs

2003   Western Union Introduces Singing Mammogram

2004   FDA Approves Nicotine Eye Patch

2005   Visa To Assume National Debt for 5.9 percent, No Annual Fee

Hair Club For Men Must Admit Women, High Court Rules	*2006*
Critic Calls Composer Karlheinz Stockhausen's Deathbed Screams "An Atonal Masterpiece"	*2007*
Emergency Gravel Transfusion Saves Rod Stewart's Voice	*2009*
"Bad Luck Gene" Identified	*2010*
New Superconductive Material Will Make Electrocutions More Entertaining	*2011*
"For God's Sake, Use A Decent Camera!" Pleads Extraterrestrial	*2012*
Turnout For Apocalypse Lighter Than Expected; Most Prefer To Be Elsewhere When World Ends	*2015*

IT'S FUNNY UNTIL SOMEONE LOSES AN EYE (THEN IT'S *Really* FUNNY)

Afterword

In his book *Sleepers Joining Hands*, the poet Robert Bly admits, "I often long for some prose when I'm reading a book of poems." I know what he means. Sometimes in the middle of a book of humor I find myself longing for something serious. If the humor writer is worth anything, I usually get it—not too much, mind you, just enough. Hopefully a bit of non-comedic commentary at the end of this volume will not try your patience, and may even help illuminate what you've just read.

In *ABC of Reading*, Ezra Pound writes, "Journalism is news. Literature is news that stays news." That's good luck for literature but usually bad luck for humor, which tends to be closer to news than to literature, and thus does not stay news, does not live beyond the time and the impulse that gave it birth. Most humor is written from a specifically topical spur: a news item, a snippet of popular culture, a current trend. It doesn't necessarily take great artistry to wring laughs from this subject matter, because instant recognition is one of the prerequisites to laughter, and the topical is by definition recognizable. But even if great artistry is involved (as, say, in the *Daily Show*), it is as transient as a Mayfly, doomed to die on the day it was born. Will the *Daily Show* still seem hysterically funny 10 years from now? Or 20? I doubt it. And that's all right. It has already served its purpose.

However, where does that leave the humor writer who hopes to create laughter that is more lasting? Is that even a realistic goal? And if so, how does one begin to achieve it?

The *Onion* has found one way to do this. Many *Onion* stories, while superficially topical, are really generic social satire dealing with permanent aspects of the human condition. That's why a lot of early *Onion* stories are still funny today.

My own solution has been similar, if hopefully more individualized than the *Onion* corporate fake news voice adopted perforce by all *Onion* staffers. When I first began reading Robert Benchley and the other early 20th century *New Yorker* humorists—still the greatest humor writers of all time, in my opinion—I carefully noted which pieces had aged well, and which had not. A piece about Shakespeare, or opera libretti, still resonates because each of those is part of the canon of Western civilization. A piece about a forgotten radio program, or a forgotten labor leader, not so much. I resolved to avoid the purely topical as much as possible, to parody only great authors, and to comment only on situations and subjects that people in any country in any decade might be able to relate to.

The result is, I hope, a true miscellany that includes parodies of great literature (Kafka, Hemingway, Hardy, Plato, etc.), parodies of artifacts familiar from daily life (a letter of recommendation, a census form, a tax form, a newspaper editorial), pieces dealing with canonical segments of culture (period songs, fake anthropology, conceptual art, and so on), pieces about science in the broad aspect (a battle between two paleontologists, a new angle on seismology, a look at the comic side of space travel), personal or relationship humor (a family vacation, a childhood memoir), and what can only be deemed pure nonsense (a Dada-like play, an American history sans history, an update on UFO's), as well as darker bits reflecting the author's own psyche and the spirit of the times (various con games, nightmares, cancer-causing horoscopes, and yes, zombies!).

These pieces were written over the better—or worse—part of a lifetime, some of them decades ago, some within the last year. If you can't tell which is which, I will already have largely succeeded according to my own definition of success. I'm not ashamed to say I had a huge amount of fun writing them, and I hope they bring you some amusement as well. As Preston Sturges has his lead character say at the end of the wonderful screwball comedy-about-comedy, *Sullivan's Travels*, "There's a lot to be said for making people laugh. Did you know that that's all some people have? It isn't much, but it's better than nothing in this cockeyed caravan."

ACKNOWLEDGEMENTS

With a book whose composition spans decades, there will be many people to thank and only the author to blame, so please, a little patience, a little indulgence. I'll be here all week, and don't forget to tip your waitress.

Let me start by thanking my parents for raising me in a house filled with books. Not just any books. Books on very conceivable subject, the odder and more exotic the better. On the wall as far as the eye could see were mostly classics, ancient and modern, famous and obscure. In their home I first encountered W.B. Yeats, Robert Frost, Jane Austen, J.R.R. Tolkien, T.E. Lawrence, Aldous Huxley, Ernest Hemingway, Ray Bradbury, Robert Heinlein, Isaac Asimov, John Collier, Muriel Spark, Evelyn Waugh, Plato, Sophocles, Alan Watts, Carl Jung, Robert Ardrey, Konrad Lorenz, H.L. Mencken, and most significantly for a future humorist, Robert Benchley, James Thurber, S.J. Perelman, Don Marquis, Dorothy Parker and P.G. Wodehouse.

My father also collected comedy albums by such American performers as Second City, Jonathan Winters, Shelley Berman, the Smothers Brothers, Bob Newhart, Bob and Ray, Lenny Bruce, and some key giants of English comedy, including the *Goon Show* (with a young Peter Sellers) and *Beyond the Fringe* (with a young Peter Cook and Dudley Moore). I'm pretty sure we were the only household in Wheaton, Illinois, that could boast both Peter Cook's *The Misty Mister Wisty* album and *The Absurd Imposters*, an impossibly rare record by Jim Coyle and Mal Sharpe. In addition my

190

father was an aficionado of Old Time Radio, initiating me into the antique audio comedy joys of Jack Benny, Fred Allen, Bob Hope, Edgar Bergen and W.C. Fields, as well as Orson Welles, Norman Corwin, Arch Oboler, and all the rest of the great radio dramatists. My very first comedy performance was before friends of my parents in the Luchs basement, leading my siblings in a loose adaptation of Oboler's *Cat Wife* redubbed *Pig Wife*. Later a drug dealing friend of my father's turned him and the rest of us on to the surreal, multilayered studio comedy records of the Firesign Theatre, the single most important influence on my becoming a humor writer.

For all of this I thank my mother and father. I also thank them for teaching me to read, at my insistence, before I enrolled in school. That set me on a lifelong path of being a confirmed autodidact. From the beginning I was keenly aware that learning was something I did myself because I could and should, because the world is brimming with mysterious marvels waiting to be explored, and there is never enough time to experience them all. Learning was never merely something that teachers did to me or imparted to me against my will.

That said, I thank my fifth grade teacher, Mrs. Francis, who did so much to encourage my appreciation of the *New Yorker* humorists and other fine authors, and who tolerated my mercifully brief attempts to compose light verse in the manner of Ogden Nash, my first feeble stab at writing humor.

When I was in my early twenties I got the dubious idea that if the world had fallen in love with the four Marx Brothers, it could fall in love with the four Luchs Brothers. We spent seven years trying to prove me right, writing and performing sketch comedy in the recording studio and on various stages, mostly in the Midwest. Our biggest success was fairly modest, and something of an anomaly. We released a Sex Pistols parody—the only one in existence, so far as I know—a 45 single called "Kill Me I'm Rotten," backed with "Losing My Lunch Over You." It sold well for a tiny independent record, especially as an import to Europe, and got airplay on Dr. Demento's syndicated radio show. Eventually it was bootlegged multiple times on such punk collections as the *Killed By Death* series. To this day, some of the few people who do remember the Luchs Brothers remember them as what they never were: a punk band. I remember, though. In particular I recall how much I learned about comedy writing and life in general by collaborating with my brothers Ernst, Helmut and Rolf. For that uniquely enriching experience, I thank them. And I thank our producer and eternal best friend, James Youker, whose ears could match George Martin's.

I heartily thank the Firesign Theatre, always the Luchs Brothers' deepest inspiration: Philip Austin, Peter Bergman, David Ossman and Philip Proctor. Ossman was in some important ways a mentor to the group and to me individually as well, and all of them became Dear Friends to one degree or another. Austin and Bergman are now gone but never forgotten.

Many thanks are due to Bill Knight, former editor of the *Prairie Sun*, the alternative Midwest newspaper that published a weekly humor column by the Luchs Brothers. Bill doubled down on this insanity when he agreed to collect the best of those columns into *The Luchs Brothers' End-of-the-World Party Book*, with a witty and affectionate introduction by David Ossman and a glorious wraparound color cover by Gahan Wilson. A few of the pieces from that book are recollected here.

Fond acknowledgement should also go the nuns who ran the Pier Coffeehouse in Wheaton, Illinois, and to Mike Franklin who ran the Colloquy Coffeehouse in Elgin, Illinois, our two most frequent local venues. Patients from the nearby Elgin state mental home would sometimes attend our Colloquy shows on a weekend pass, laughing at everything about five seconds too late and throwing off our timing. In addition I would like to thank Emo Philips for often sharing those stages and others with us, and for his encouragement over the years.

After the end of the Luchs Brothers I was exhausted and discouraged. I abandoned all creative efforts for about a decade. The time was not a complete waste as I spent most of it reading thousands of books and educating myself on any number of topics. Don't get me started on multiverse theory! In time, though, I was to become a parent, and it occurred to me that my children deserved the example of a father who had not given up on his dreams. With the aid of a talented counselor, the late Jim Cassens, whom I could never thank enough on either side of the grave, I got my head on straight (it had been turned backwards ever since I saw *The Exorcist*) and back into the game.

Following up on a lead from Emo Philips, I got in touch with the *Onion*, the satirical publication then just embarking on its rapid rise to fame. Thus began a nearly two-decade association that proved creatively exhilarating and professionally profitable. I contributed both to the paper and to many of the *Onion* books, such as *Our Dumb Century*, winner of the Thurber Prize for humor. I owe a tremendous debt of appreciation to the *Onion* and the many editors I worked with there, especially founder Scott Dikkers, Carol Kolb and Rob Siegel. Rob was my main weekly contact in those early days, and a more generous and helpful soul it would be impossible to find.

Among other benefits, working with the *Onion* also afforded me the visibility and opportunity to write comedy for television, where so many *Onion* veterans have migrated. I am grateful to Bill Maher and his head writer Chris Kelly for hiring me at *Politically Incorrect* and thereby getting me into the Writer's Guild. My single season with that show ended all too quickly, and I am thankful to Craig Kilborn and his head writer Billy Kimball for immediately inviting me to write for the *Late Late Show*, a very enjoyable gig that lasted much longer. Eventually through that connection I was headhunted by a radio comedy enterprise called the Complete Sheet—thank you, Complete Sheet! -- and then by a similar enterprise called American Comedy Network, where I spent six delightful years working alongside one of the best comedy talents in the radio business, Joel Graham. I learned so much simply by being around him, and that job was really more fun than anyone should be allowed to have at work.

Another reason I need to thank Chris Kelly is that he introduced me to *McSweeney's Internet Tendency*, the online humor publication started by Dave Eggers. A number of the pieces in this book first appeared there. *McSweeney's* was also the inspiration for my own literary humor site *The Big Jewel*, and for countless others. Dave can't help being an inspirational guy. I thank him for that, and for letting me share the stage with him in Boston and elsewhere on the madcap reading tour for the *McSweeney's* anthology *Created in Darkness by Troubled Americans*.

Speaking of anthologies and the peculiar people who make them, thanks to Michael J. Rosen, editor of the anthology *May Contain Nuts*, and to Amy Vansant, editor of the anthology *Moms Are Nuts*, for including me. As I recall, Newton's Fourth Law states that every humor anthology must bear a title with the word "nuts" in it somewhere. Further thanks are owed to Barnes and Noble and the good folks at Becker-Mayer for publishing my book, *Leave the Gun, Take the Cannoli: A Wiseguy's Guide to the Workplace*.

Thanks to Yale University, Wheaton College, Western Illinois University, Baylor University, and the other institutions of higher learning that have invited me to lecture about comedy and humor writing. Now, all of you other denizens of academia, what are you waiting for? Lecture bureaus? Agents? Anyone? Crickets, a sound well known to humorists. Call me!

I would like to thank my colleagues past and present at *The Big Jewel* literary humor site (thebigjewel.com), among them cofounder Neil Pasricha, and my current editorial crew of Becky Cardwell, Whitney Collins, Ralph Gamelli, David Jaggard and Tyler Smith, as well as webmaster Amy Vansant, and the hundreds of brilliant humor writers from around the world who have contributed since we launched this handmade boat in May of 2002. David Jaggard also copy edited this manuscript, though I hasten to add that I am solely responsible for any errors and infelicities still remaining.

I owe a very special thank you to Jacob Smullyan of Sagging Meniscus Press for giving this collection such a good home. His early enthusiasm and continual encouragement have made this project a delight to work on. I am proud to be in the company of his other authors.

Finally, I wish to thank Roberta Laine for being the unexpected love of my life, and my daughters, Nora and Jia, for being the best things I have ever helped bring into this world, better than any humor piece I ever wrote.

Grateful acknowledgment is made to the following publications and their editors for first publishing the pieces collected in this book, most of which have since been revised and improved: *The Big Jewel, Gander Press Review, Kugelmass, LitWit, McSweeney's Internet Tendency, Modern Humorist, Moms Are Nuts* (anthology), *Monkeybicycle, The New Satirist, The New Yorker, Pindeldyboz, POP, The Prairie Sun, Rational Review, Slate, The Talking Mirror, Yankee Pot Roast.*

About the Author

Kurt Luchs has written humor all of his life for nearly every medium. He has contributed to such prominent humor outlets as the *Onion, the New Yorker* and *McSweeney's Internet Tendency*. His work has been represented in most of the Onion books, including *Our Dumb Century*, winner of the Thurber Prize for humor, and in a number of anthologies, including *May Contain Nuts* (Harper-Collins), *Created in Darkness by Troubled Americans* (Knopf/Random House) and *Moms Are Nuts* (Vansant Creations). Barnes and Noble published his book *Leave the Gun, Take the Cannoli: A Wiseguy's Guide to the Workplace*, a collection of gangster movie quotes and commentary applied to best practices. In television, he has written comedy for Bill Maher at *Politically Incorrect* and Craig Kilborn at the *Late Late Show*. In radio, he was a staff writer for the comedy prep service the Complete Sheet, and later for American Comedy Network, which he also managed. Since 2002 he has edited and frequently contributed to *The Big Jewel*, a leading site for literary humor, which he co-founded. As a member of the sibling comedy troupe the Luchs Brothers, he co-wrote and sang the independent hit novelty single "Kill Me I'm Rotten," the world's first (and still only) Sex Pistols parody, which was featured on the Dr. Demento syndicated radio show and has been officially re-released and bootlegged several times. The Luchs Brothers' original WWII propaganda parody script, *Dirk Scabbard—Home Front Hero*, won the American Radio Theater scriptwriting contest. Kurt Luchs also writes poetry, which he has published in such publications as *Former People Journal, Into the Void, Minetta Review, Poydras Re-*

view, *Triggerfish Critical Review, Otis Nebula, Sheila-Na-Gig, Right Hand Pointing, Roanoke Review, Wilderness House Literary Review, Crosswinds Poetry Journal, Grey Sparrow Journal, Noctua Review, Quail Bell Magazine, Antiphon, Light, Phantom Drift, Fjords Review, Verse-Virtual, The Ibis Head Review,* and *Burningword Literary Journal,* among others. He is preparing to publish his first volume of poems, tentatively titled *One of These Things Is Not Like the Other.* In addition, he is currently writing an autobiographical novel with the working title of *Honey Street,* under the theory that because it's a novel, no one will be able to sue him.